KT-179-999

9030 00006 7004 7

FROM THE WRECK

From The Wreck

JANE RAWSON

PICADOR

First published 2017 by Transit Lounge Publishing, Melbourne, Australia

First published in the UK 2019 by Picador
an imprint of Pan Macmillan
20 New Wharf Road, London N1 9RR
Associated companies throughout the world
www.panmacmillan.com

ISBN 978-1-5290-0654-4

Copyright © Jane Rawson 2017

The right of Jane Rawson to be identified as the
author of this work has been asserted by her in accordance
with the Copyright, Designs and Patents Act 1988.

All rights reserved. No part of this publication may be reproduced,
stored in a retrieval system, or transmitted, in any form, or by any means
(electronic, mechanical, photocopying, recording or otherwise)
without the prior written permission of the publisher.

Pan Macmillan does not have any control over, or any responsibility for,
any author or third-party websites referred to in or on this book.

1 3 5 7 9 8 6 4 2

A CIP catalogue record for this book is available from the British Library.

Printed and bound by CPI Group (UK) Ltd, Croydon, CR0 4YY

This book is sold subject to the condition that it shall not, by way of
trade or otherwise, be lent, hired out, or otherwise circulated without
the publisher's prior consent in any form of binding or cover other than
that in which it is published and without a similar condition including
this condition being imposed on the subsequent purchaser.

Visit www.picador.com to read more about all our books
and to buy them. You will also find features, author interviews and
news of any author events, and you can sign up for e-newsletters
so that you're always first to hear about our new releases.

For Soren Holm
and for Tane

LONDON BOROUGH OF WANDSWORTH	
9030 00006 7004 7	
Askews & Holts	18-Apr-2019
AF SF	£14.99
	WW19000290

Many of the parrots, monkeys, and other animals we had on board, were already burnt or suffocated; but several had retreated to the bowsprit out of reach of the flames, appearing to wonder what was going on, and quite unconscious of the fate that awaited them. We tried to get some of them into the boats, by going as near as we could venture; but they did not seem at all aware of the danger they were in, and would not make any attempt to reach us. As the flames caught the base of the bowsprit, some of them ran back and jumped into the midst of the fire.

Alfred Russell Wallace, *Narrative of Travels on the Amazon and Rio Negro*

But I, awakened from sleep, considered in my excellent heart whether to drop from the deck and die right there in the sea or endure, keep silent, go on being one of the living.

Homer, *Odyssey*

THE WRECK

1

He felt it first when the horses shifted and cried. They had been muttering among themselves all day, but this was different, a note of panic in it. *The horses aren't yours to care about, George,* he reminded himself. He went from cabin to cabin and collected the crockery and cutlery smeared and encrusted with an early dinner, the passengers getting ready for bed.

Jupiter. He'd heard them call the horse Jupiter. He could hear the horses nickering and wondered why it was that everything felt a little off. *I'll leave this cleaning just one moment,* he thought, *and go below. I'll just make sure someone is attending to them and then I'll return to the galley.*

'Jupiter.' He breathed the name out because there was no one there, only the six horses and George himself. 'Jupiter,' but no horse turned his head to look. He didn't know which among them was the famous racer. They were shuffling still, something anxious about them. He told himself, *You know nothing of horses, what do you mean something anxious, how would you know?* But he felt his own sweat prick a little.

He sat himself on a flour barrel and watched the horses nudge one another, the flick of their tails. He may have closed his eyes. He did not think he had. But when he opened them there was another, a woman. She was running her finger around the rim of the horse's mouth and it stood, death-still, eyelids peeled back and eyes locked on her shadowed face. She leaned forward out of the darkness and licked the foam from the horse's quivering muzzle and George could hear the creature breathe, a strange whimper deep in its chest. That did not sound like comfort. 'Harvesting' was the word that forced itself to George's mind.

He stood as slowly and quietly as he could and left the enclosure back-first. The floor creaked but she did not once raise her eyes to him, nor did the horse shift its stare from her face.

He returned to the galley and the cleaning he'd abandoned. There were eighteen women on board and he had served each of them dinner during the evening. That woman had not been among them. *But you did not see her face,* he reminded himself. *And you are only one day out from Port Adelaide — how can you be so sure you know your passengers well enough to recognise one in the darkness, in an unexpected place?*

There were steps behind him and a hand sliding into the

crack of his arse: Mason, of course. The assistant steward cackled loudly as George turned to flick him with the wet dishcloth.

'You'll have a brandy with us, won't you, Hills? Finish that up and come have a brandy.'

George packed the last of the crockery away and cast the woman from his mind.

The other stewards and a couple of the able seamen were packed around a table in an empty aft cabin. Davey Peters, too, the fireman George had travelled with the last four or five times. Not Mrs Meagher, though; she preferred to stay up front, where the company was 'higher quality'.

Mason slid a glass over to him and asked what he thought of the horseflesh.

'Horseflesh?' Had someone seen him visiting the horses below?

'The sheilas, man. Seen a decent set of catheads among 'em?' Mason asked.

'All mothers and wan spinsters back our way, aren't they, George? Not much chop at all,' said O'Brien, who'd been handling the aft cabins alongside George that evening.

'Haven't seen a one as wouldn't splinter to bits under the weight of me,' George confirmed, and it was true: they were a feeble-looking bunch. 'Still, as long as they could hold it together for the duration, I wouldn't complain if they expired after.'

Mason cackled – it only took the slightest provocation – and poured him another.

'There is one up front, though,' Peters said, 'much more your style, Georgie. Big, plump pair on her, arse like a pumpkin.'

'Blonde?' George asked.

'Brunette as they come. What do they call it? Mahogany or somesuch.'

He did like a strong, plump brunette.

'Big girl, is she?'

'Ooh, I've really caught your attention, haven't I? Nope, not above five four, I'd say, but plenty of meat on her bones.'

George's Eliza appeared before him, her shining brown hair and adorable chubby backside, and he reminded her he'd be back to marry her soon, he just had one or two more trips to make, a few more coins to save, another girl or two – adventurous, entangled elsewhere; he didn't like the lonely types – to tumble.

And though he'd cast her from his mind, he did see her again, fleetingly, that apparition among the horses. Had she been brown-headed? A set of rounded handfuls? All he had left of her was a creeping sense of dread; nothing physical he could call to mind.

'Ledwith, her name is,' said Mason.

'Oh, how do you know, you big show-off?' the cabin boy blurted out, and someone threw a cushion at his head and told him to pipe down.

'It is,' Mason said. 'Bridget Ledwith. She was down below, wandering around, and I asked her did she need a helping hand' – he mimed groping her arse – 'was she lost, and she told me all chilly that no thank you she was just fine. I followed her back to her cabin anyway, just in case. Got her name off the door.'

'Down below?' George asked.

'Trust you to pick that up, Hills,' Peters laughed, and George laughed with him, remembering suddenly the mouth on the woman and thinking what she might be able to do with it.

Between them they finished that bottle and then another one and there were only a few more hours until they all had to be back on deck. George looked around him and saw that only Mason and he and the cabin boy, asleep on the floor, were left.

'Enough,' he said, and Mason agreed. It was a stumbling walk back to their quarters, made longer when George declared he was just going above to piss off the edge.

'Have one for me,' Mason said, and veered off towards bed.

Just a small look, George thought to himself. *Just a peek. And if she's worth it, then tomorrow I'll be all charm. Might even comb the old locks,* he thought.

All the stewards knew how to come and go, unobtrusive, so it was nothing for George to gently slide open the door of

Miss Ledwith's cabin, to adjust his eyes to the dark and scan her sleeping form for flaws and favours. There were many points in her advantage, Mason was right, but there was one thing she was not, and that was the woman George had seen below. The shape of her was the same; the colouring too – it all came back to him in a rush. But when he saw her he did not feel death behind him and the cold pit of the sea floor.

It's the brandy speaking, George, he told himself. *Cold pit of the sea floor, indeed. Bed now, and a smidge of sleep, then tomorrow a play for this flossie.* But still he couldn't shake the sight of her, her lips against the horse's foaming mouth.

*

He had slept, perhaps, for two hours, then arisen to prepare the ladies' breakfasts.

At the inquiry, months later, he heard that some time on that first evening one of the horses had fallen, knocked from its feet by the rough seas. The racer's owner had demanded a shift in course and the captain had turned the prow of the ship into the swell to ease its heaving. Had it brought about the wreck, this shift? Perhaps. It did not occur to George to stand and say that it was something other than the swell that had caused the horses to panic. He didn't even believe it himself.

Instead he had told the inquiry, blunt but polite, that he

did not know the cause, he did not hold blame; that all he could say was eight days, eight nights was too long to spend half-submerged in the freezing Southern Ocean with little food and no water and with the dead and the sharks ever increasing in the bloody waters around. But whose fault was it? He didn't know. Perhaps the lifeboat could have come sooner: it seemed it had tried. He was thanked and dismissed with no further questions because it was clear to everyone he had nothing more to add.

He had a great deal more to add, and none of it on that particular topic. He would have liked to ask the court how it was possible that the woman Bridget Ledwith had changed her form so utterly from one day to the next. He would have enquired how was it she had seen into every part of him those eight days and eight nights but now he could see nothing of her because she was gone. Vanished. They mentioned her in the course of the hearing, certainly, but as though it was no great mystery for a grown woman to go missing, to disappear entirely from the colony's face. Privacy, they said, or something; a lady's right to be left alone.

Also, he would have liked to say, how did such a little wreck, such a gentle wreck, break, ruin and drown the lives of so many? He had not even noticed when the ship first lifted and dropped onto the reef. One drop of coffee had spilled from the pot he was carrying to the ladies' cabins for breakfast service; he could see, clear in his mind, that drop as it rolled across the timber below his feet and he felt the shuddering mass of the boat slow, settle, creak to a halt. *Why have we stopped?* he'd thought. *We've arrived already?* But before the thought had even completed itself he saw an enormous wave wash over the companionway, taking men, women and children to the bottom with barely a chance to scream.

He couldn't say for sure that even then he'd realised the ship was sinking. He had dropped the pot and rushed to his cabin to find his savings. Is that something a man does on the brink of death? Perhaps it is. He'd thrust the money in his pocket, and by the time he'd made his way up top, the boat had begun in earnest to tear itself apart.

George had hauled himself over the broken bulwarks, tearing his back to shreds, dodged between the hoofs of maddened race horses stampeding about the deck, scrambled into the rigging of the main mast, where a phenomenal wave washed over the lines where he was clinging, and both he and the mast were swept into the ocean. He could still see, always somewhere behind his eyes, that monstrous wave rushing towards him, its foamy head hanging above him, then the blue-black-green crashing upon him, filling his lungs and mind with blank, white, drowning fear.

God, the despair when his trousers, with his savings in the pocket, were torn from him and swept out to sea. *All that bloody stewarding for nothing,* he'd thought, forgetting for the moment he would probably be dead before ten minutes was up. *All that yes ma'am no ma'am right away ma'am and now I haven't got a damn bit to show for it and I might as well drown myself this second. Twenty-four bloody years old and nothing at all to show for myself.* He was in space, it seemed; flying through space. The bottom of the mast had got stuck in something and now the top, with him attached, was thrashing itself about in the air. George had always hated the circus and this did not strike him as particularly funny. Hurtling through space with a naked arse he looked towards the ship, expecting a laughing crowd arrayed on the deck, and he'd been surprised to see a mess of floating, splintered lumber, a wet and screaming array of bodies, where once his ship had been. He fell back into the water beside one of the bigger chunks.

That young bloke, Soren Holm, just come from Denmark, reached down and pulled him from the water. George was wearing one shoe and a belt. He felt a body pressed beside him, softer than his own. He turned his head and saw it was her, but with a dampness and coldness about her that told him here, at last, was the woman he had seen below. 'Miss Ledwith,' he said, though he knew she wasn't, and he felt her small, clinging hand slip inside his.

The sun was just beginning to rise.

2

One eye open, then the other.

Am I still me? I touch here, taste this, smell that. I remember. I am still me. One thing holding fast in this shifting, blurring mass.

But the rest of it? None of the shapes are right. Is that a life form? Is that? There is neither the sight nor feel of wrapped-tight energy, of breathing hot, of burning fuel, of soul-filled bursting selfness that is like anyone I have ever seen. I don't even know who to eat.

I will sit slumping cold and starving here, in this cave, in this wet puddle of an ocean. Who would even mark my death? That crusty-shelled little nobody over there? That slippery piece of meat and teeth? I don't think so. Weren't we supposed to be a once-proud race of warriors? I flail at the memory of us and the hurt of it tears strips from me and I decide I can't remember. Still, I am certain we were not the type whose deaths were marked by becoming passing food for some slippery piece of meat and teeth.

No, not that.

I may be me but I know how not to look it. I put one small part of me out of my cave and make it the shape of the sand. I watch it and squint my eyes and I think, yes, sand. So I put another small part of me out there to join the first. Still sandy. With five parts out and three in I suddenly feel ashamed as though maybe another of my people can see this cringing cowardice and the rest pours out and I'm all there, out of the cave, and I am as good as sand. I roll my eyes up down left right and feel the flavours around with every feeling part of me and nothing is there ready to eat me but nor are there any of my people laughing at my doltish slow transformation into what maybe is sand. I move, slow-shifting, sand-like, across the land until I meet rock and then I am shifting even slower, rock-shaped and rock-like, but oh rock moves so slow so slow and so I have to take the shape of another. I sit, rock-like, and watch first this one then another cruise by until I have a library of forms and movements and I am all shifting life forms behind my eyes. I try that one, slow floater with grey-green strands and I am it, letting go of the rock I slow-float strands, swimming the currents around me.

Something goes by and so I eat it. At least the crunch of tiny bones is familiar when all else is strange. Here some star is oozing warmth and light. There are shards and vivid jangles; shadows smear the outlines of things. I smear my own, slide a little higher – through this colour and that, one smooth, one sharp, one altogether knobbly – always towards the heat of that star. It is tender and tentative on the skin of me, barely warm, barely more yellow than grey. I spread myself flatwise to make the most of it. I stretch and thin my shape, I slide myself up this rough rocky form and that, and find myself in another kind of air altogether.

It is dry and it is bright. There is a crashing, pounding, smashing sound and I hear it in my ears and then I hear it in my whole body. I do not want to be here or there or anywhere but only then and past and previous. Not now. Nowhere and nowhen that ocean strikes shore.

I tumble back, in: under. I tumble back under, down, down, down. I am a rock that plummets back to the sandy floor. I am a rock that rolls – and no I don't care how – into the mouth of this cave to stop and breathe and sorrow. I make myself me. One wet ball of hate and homesickness, I take the shape of fury and grief and hopeless, hopeless, hopeless.

I sit. I wait. I think.

Once upon a time there was a world all ocean. It fell wet across the whole world, nothing but water. The water was fat with life and with death. It had been this way always, though of course once it had been ice, a brittle ball of crisp blue-white with life squeezed into the tiniest corners and cracks, fidgeting its way to warmth for thousands and thousands and millions of years.

Once upon a time the globe stretched its crumpled warming tentacles and ice melted to water. This life form got bigger and this one got smaller, harder or softer or a few extra tendrils until every niche on the whole wet ball of it was full of the creature that had evolved to be there. And for thousands and thousands and millions of years, that was what we did.

So many creatures were bigger than we were, and so many had more teeth. But we were built for thinking, for making, for talking. We could squeeze into any space. We could shift into any shape. And that was who we were and what we did: we didn't fight the others to be bigger, fiercer, more toothy. We were evidently us.

We knew the place we lived. We came to know other places – other planets, other dimensions. Places that were just like home but not quite; times that were nothing like this at all and even beyond anything we could imagine or understand. We found a billion realities where we could be so impossible as to cease existing.

Aeon after aeon we explored it, stretched our shapes into other life forms across a million years and a million places, times and ways of being. We found there was no place like home. A planet all ocean. We sank ourselves back into the soft waters and vowed to always stay.

They came out of the sky, tumbling through our atmosphere and dropping into the sea. Their ship bobbed about. We thought they were just curious and that soon they'd be gone.

They stayed. More showed up. Many, many more. They built machines, giant, and chemical plants. They built walls in the water and broke the ocean into seas and then they pushed the seas aside. They filled the spaces with dirt and their big dirty footprints got bigger and bigger and bigger until our all-ocean world became a world half land. The ocean broke upon the shore.

Now there wasn't space enough to hold us. Now there weren't creatures enough to feed us. Not enough niches to go around and no one sure anymore whose niche was whose anyway. We fought each other and we fought them.

They moved us like they moved the water. They filled in our ocean. They murdered us by accident and by design. They won and we lost and there were so, so few of us left and so we fled. We launched ourselves out into that great quiet space. We listened to nothing but the thrum of stars for I don't know how long. We tumbled into another time, space, dimension.

I crawled into this cave.

I don't know how long I've been here and I have no idea how long I can last. Is there anyone left?

I sleep. I catch and eat and sometimes it is slippery and

others the crunch of tiny bones. I will not die here. One part of me, then another then the next, becomes sand and I am once again on my way. Sliding sand, slow floater with grey-green strands, this time the darting stripes of some intrepid speedster, then rock again and rock and rest. The sun, that star. No resting in that meagre light this time. Too much time at rest and I will lose my nerve.

Above it is turmoil. Water in great towers and sheets, pushed to mountains by the freezing wind. A great grey-green howl of it. Chunks and spars of scaly and slimy and once-was-tree, all tumbled about. I fix myself fast to one and let it go where it will. We go and go and go and I couldn't say if it's towards or away from whatever it is I had meant to be doing here in this better life. It's darker, the one star gone - the sun, that bully – but all the rest are still there, I see, now they have a chance to show their faces. I bathe in their hum and sing the song of my people and it drops frail into the sea, no other ears to hear.

We smash now against another, swift and looming, and I move on.

I am the shape of the wood now and all about me is the shape of the sea. I cling and spread and make my way higher until I find a place that is closed and dark and for now I rest.

I sleep.

When I wake there is a smell so gigantic I hear it as a noise pounding on my brain. The world is full of animal:

hard smashing feet and white rolling eyes and this is not a good place to be soft and floor-bound.

I wait, small and dark. Squeezed into a dry corner I make myself the feel the look of wood and keep my softness clear of the smash of feet. I watch for a shape I could be. Others come and go, one or two, brown and upright and with a lot of whispering hush between themselves and the foot-smashers. They cart and carry things, they provide food and try to scrape away a little of the smell. Could I be one like this? They feel so very present, so obvious, and I have put my bravery away somewhere and can't quite remember how to find it.

Another comes and it is upright too but smaller, quieter and also brighter, blues and yellows, greens sprinkled across itself. It performs no tasks. It murmurs to itself and maybe to the foot-smashers, but they do not heed it the way they do the browner types. It is shadow-bound and ignored and it slips away again without any type of notice.

This I could try.

I remember how the creature looked and squeeze myself to the boundaries of its shape, approximate myself to its tentacles and tendrils and colours. None of it is quite entirely right but perhaps it is good enough that I can eat and not be eaten.

The feet have stopped with their smashing. Those creatures stand quiet now and I sit, the way my model did, and watch them. I murmur in a way I hope will pass. But though I am shadow-bound, I am not ignored. They stare at me and roll their big white eyes and over them a dampness spreads. 'You are bringing the sea inside,' I tell them. 'What tiny oceans are these?' I move to them and dip my extremities in their moistened hides, taste their salt. They are not soothed.

'Small creatures,' I tell them, because aren't we all? 'Small creatures, calm yourselves.' We taste each other's breath and they know there's none of their kind been through my mouth and they still themselves. Small creatures. We talk, this and that. Minds only; no sounds. They are the feel of speed squeezed into muscle and bone. They show me their terrible smashing feet pushing hard against grassy ground, an ocean of sweat, blood so loud in their ears they can't hear a single other thing.

Someone has come, silent, making our seven into eight. I don't turn to look but I feel it, another of those brown uprights, it hides quiet in the shadow and doesn't seem to want to bite. These hard-foots feel no fear so I ignore it too. When it's all done and I understand the taste of bladey-green after a high-speed chase, and they've felt the way it is to tumble like a rock to the very bottom of everything, I leave these creatures and go up into the air.

Some time in the darkest part of it, just before light returns, there is a scraping and a shuddering and we stop and we do not go. Sounds come out of the mouths of all of them, no longer a muttering and mumbling now, but a screeching and howling that tells me we are done with sleeping for the moment. Water comes in among us. Our wooden home is crumpled and bent, split into three. All of us are ocean-dwelling creatures now.

I watch the smash-footed creatures, the speed lovers, the grass croppers. They try to stay afloat but this is not their habitat. My first friends in this ecosystem and they are gone and I am sad.

One of those brown uprights, though, has found me and seems friendly. Not brown anymore so much as pink, he is, and grey sometimes. They do not like the cold. Our wooden house has become mostly sticks and we perch on them above the waves. Around us perch others and their skin too grows purple and bumped and the waves crash over us and over and over and over. Some of the perchers drop and some try to float and do for a little. Then they sink. I see the one I made myself from slide by, her blues and greens and yellows billowing under waves, pulling her down and down to the deep ocean floor.

This does not seem a good place for them, these uprights, and I wonder why they do not leave. Here the food is wet, cold and alive and speeds past too fast for their clumsy tentacles though why they don't even try to grasp it I do not know. There is the slippery stuff too, green and floaty, that hovers just below us and well within reach, but none try for that either. I have seen some of them – only when the sun, that star, is looking the other way – peel a little meat from one of their purpled companions now gone cold and still. But that is not enough for sustenance.

I don't mind it here for now. The cold has never bothered me. Nor the wet, obviously. And this one curls himself into me and snuggles against me all damp. I've taken the pinker shape that seems in favour, let go my greens and blues, so our pink shapes make a purpling blob together here in the middle of a cold, cold sea. We taste each other's breath and I try to talk with him, minds only, but he cannot hear. So back to the tasting, the tentacles, the making of a damp and snuggly blob. I cannot learn a great deal about him this way but still it is better than alone in a cave. I stay.

Each day the sun, that star, puts its dumb wan face over one, two, three fewer. Each night we see those million billion other stars. I bathe in their hum and sing the song of my people and again it drops frail into the sea, no other ears to hear. Then once more the sun, and again we are grown smaller. A few float without sinking and others become food for those slippery bits of meat with teeth. This will be the last worldly place for these uprights, those scattered still around me, and I hold the one beside me and try to think him onward into peace. 'Small creature,' I tell him, and I dream him a dream of the endless sky, the hum of the stars, a world all ocean, an eternity of dark. I dream him a dream and press the very edges of myself to his to bring him calm. But he stares still, lost and trapped in the shell of himself.

A tossed wooden vessel packed with browns and greys comes up beside us and they lift us in and off we go, farewell to our ocean home. They wrap us in cloths and mutter little noises, then my friend goes one way and I go another and once more I am alone. My cold wet cave tugs at me but I am beginning to find again those scraps of bravery so I take a smaller form, closer to the ground, four-legged and fine-whiskered, soft-pawed, sharp-clawed, and I raise my tail like a flag and slip out into this world to see what is what.

LIFE ON LAND

1

William talked on and on and George felt a hideous discomfort bubble in the guts of him. Cannibalism, William was saying now. What of it? George fidgeted on his cushion, tried to concentrate. That cannibalism might better fit a man to life. 'Not so implausible,' William was saying, smiling, man of science he was.

They'd had beef for dinner, hadn't they? Corned beef. Some vegetables. Why was William talking about cannibalism? George stared into his claret for a moment, smiled at his sister-in-law Sarah, put his pipe down and smoothed his trousers. A breath in – slow – then out; he turned to her husband, asked, 'What are you saying, exactly?'

From his reading of Darwin, William said. Charles Darwin. His reading, his understanding, was there was no such thing as morality. Nothing in and of itself good, only fit for purpose, for living and thriving wherever it was the thing found itself.

'And so cannibalism? What you're saying is?' asked George, wondering why William would always use ten words when one would do.

'That should humans be the most widely available meat, eating the flesh of humans would be the best response to such availability.'

Oh, now he saw. George knew what William was poking at. The bubble solidified into something obsidian-cool, rubbed smooth and sharp-edged in the year after year. George weighed it in his palm, tested its blade, pocketed it. Said, instead, that this would be true, surely, only if you'd nothing else to eat, yes?

'Well, not necessarily,' replied William. 'Humans, remember, are constantly at hand. Perhaps a person best suited to eating other humans would be also best suited to thrive.'

'Apart from the law, of course. Eliza, dear, do you think we need another log for the fire?' Sarah asked.

Eliza continued working on her cross-stitch but nodded at her sister. 'One moment.'

William said that this was a discussion about biology, not the frail paper of human law, and if Darwin was right, 'laws stand between us and our reaching a higher state of humanity.' George saw the man's buttocks rise out of his chair a little as he declaimed.

'That's disgusting. Eat one another if you must, but

I would rather have cheese,' Sarah said, and went to the kitchen to look for some.

'It's not that I want to eat George,' her husband called after her. 'At least, I am discussing it only as a matter of theory. I am not actually suggesting that we should become cannibals.' He turned back, smiling glibly, while George thumbed the dark bead inside, tried to keep his calm under cover of keeping his pipe alight. 'A thought experiment. Isn't that right, George?'

'So this Darwin,' George said, shaking out his match, shaking out the creases in his voice, 'he's saying you'd be a smart man, wise, to eat another bloke? Better fit to be a man than another who turns his nose up at human meat?' George could see his wife Eliza from the corner of his eye but she hadn't flinched and he wondered why it was he always thought people could see inside him, see the monster lurking there.

'Well, Darwin does not say that precisely. He doesn't concern himself with morals. I am merely ...'

George interrupted. 'Forget morals. Is he saying the cannibal is better fitted, is a more fully formed man?'

'Well, George, he didn't speak specifically on this matter.' William shifted a little in his seat, stopped talking for a second and George was pleased to see him just the slightest bit on edge, just for a moment. It was only a moment. 'I am extrapolating. But it does seem that if one takes his arguments at face value, then you could conclude … Say, if you, George, were to eat a man in circumstances where no other food was available, and due to that to go on and breed rather than die and have all your possible progeny die with you, then indeed, cannibalism would prove you the fittest and most appropriate to survive. Those who chose to abstain and therefore condemn their children to non-existence would, on the other hand, have proven themselves inadequate for the task of life.'

'And where is God in this?' Eliza asked. She knelt before the fire and took the poker from its stand. 'You would survive in this life but surely condemn your mortal soul. Thirty or forty more years of life, beautiful children, but then an eternity in hell?'

'Well, yes, there is always that to look forward to,' George muttered.

'Eliza!' William sprang from his chair. 'Let me do that. You must sit!' He grasped the poker from her hand and took the log she had placed on the hearth. 'Sit, dear, do, please. My apologies, Eliza – making you fetch wood in your state is unforgivable.'

Eliza settled herself again in the straight-backed chair before the fire. 'The Bible tells us we shouldn't put today's riches ahead of the prospect of heaven – surely eating another man in order to survive, or even have one's children survive, is worse than exploiting one's fellow man for money?

If Mister Darwin really does support such an idea, I think someone should be speaking out against him. Do you not think so, George?'

George's heart crinkled black against every person in the room. He let the cold smoke of it curl out into the kitchen to also wrap his wife's sister, happy to eat his cheese but too slow to bring it in here and stop this infernal questioning. He smiled and opened his mouth.

William interrupted before George could answer. 'Of course, Eliza, Mister Darwin says no such thing. His work is confined to the past, to attempting to explain how the creatures we see around us today came to be. He does not speak of moral dilemmas, nor does he attempt to rewrite God's law. It is merely my own foolishness, trying to apply sensible and well-thought-out science to our modern society. If anyone should be spoken out against, it is me, for drawing your wise and measured husband into such a foolish conversation!'

'No, William, no – I am interested.' George gritted his teeth, grinned at William through them, tried to relax his face. 'You do not impose.'

'But perhaps another topic of discussion.' William turned an imploring eye to his wife. 'Sarah?'

Sarah had fetched her sister a cup of tea and was now perched on the arm of a sofa, making her way through a small plate of cheese and a glass of porter. 'I was speaking this morning with Missus Higgs,' she began.

'The baker's wife?' her husband interrupted.

'The very same.'

'That does remind me, dear,' said William, 'that Mister Higgs was telling me the other day that he had heard old Jeremy Swanforth has given up his position.'

'At the Sailors' Home?' Eliza spoke up.

William nodded, swallowing the cheese he'd stolen from his wife's plate. 'Too frail to continue his duties, Mister Higgs said. He's going to live with his daughter in Portland …'

George stopped listening, began instead to wonder about this daughter. He hadn't known Swanforth had a daughter in Portland. The lifeboat had taken them there: Portland. He jammed a finger into his mouth, tried to dislodge a string of meat caught between two back teeth. He hadn't been back there since, to Portland. William was still talking.

'… near burned the place to the ground last month when he fell asleep smoking.'

'I see,' Eliza said and turned to look at George. He smiled and gave her an encouraging nod. Whatever it was she had wanted from him, she did not press the point. She turned back to look at the fire and he continued worrying at the shred of meat.

'At any rate,' William was saying, 'what was that you said about Missus Higgs, dear?'

'She claimed to be in mourning, though I must say I saw no sign of it. For Australia's greatest poet,' Sarah said.

'Not Carboni!' George was taken aback by the anguish that flickered on William's ironic face.

'Who?'

'The hero of the Eureka! Raffaello Carboni! Who, indeed.' William crossed his arms and sank back in his chair. 'Well, at least it was not him. Who then?'

'Adam Lindsay Gordon.'

'Gordon? That hack! What's to mourn?'

'I rather enjoy his work,' said Eliza, and George saw the sweet corners of her mouth turn up as she recited, '"Life is mostly froth and bubble, Two things stand like stone, Kindness in another's trouble, Courage in your own."'

'You see?' William retorted.

'How did he die?' Eliza asked.

'His own hand, I fear,' Sarah replied.

'Oh the poor man!' cried Eliza. 'Surely things were not so bad. He had a gift.'

'Financial troubles, Missus Higgs said. And pain. Too many riding accidents.'

'Courage in your own, indeed,' said William.

Sarah ignored him.

'That reef,' George said, and let the stones of it rattle around his mouth.

'I'm sorry, George?' Sarah turned to him.

'Look sharp.' He hadn't meant to yell. 'A large vessel lies jamm'd on the reef, And many on board still, and some wash'd on shore. Ride straight with the news – they may send some relief from the township; and we – we can do little more.'

'*From the Wreck,* isn't it?' Sarah replied. 'Didn't Gordon ride to Gambier Town to raise the alarm?'

'He was in Robe,' George said. 'Nowhere near.'

'Still, the event clearly stuck in his heart,' Sarah said.

'And for his efforts, he was paid back with poverty, sorrow and death by his own hand. Three cheers for Carpenters Reef.' George gulped the rest of his claret.

Eliza rose from her chair, but George, who really had not expected to be yelling tonight, reached out his hand to stop her. He patted his chest, felt his warm human self there, touched the arm of his warm human wife. 'My beautiful wife,' he murmured, 'carrying our first child.' He took the pieces of his face and shaped them into a smile for her, then turned it upon her sister, her sister's husband. He reached again for the decanter. 'Don't mind me,' he said.

'We should go,' Sarah said. 'It is late – it is no wonder you are tired. Eliza, thank you so much for dinner.'

'Yes, yes, certainly,' William added. 'Apologies to you, George, Eliza, for keeping you so long from your beds with idle chitchat.'

'No, do not go,' George said. 'I am much better now. William –' he had succeeded in refilling his glass and pushed the decanter in his brother-in-law's direction – 'What of the mill?' George felt his human self solidify, sentences forming clean and functional in his brain. 'What was the thing you were telling me about? Barking? A new barking … uh …' but the word escaped him.

'Ah, now there's a thing!' William reached for the wine. 'I was speaking to the foreman – you know Jameson?'

George nodded though he had no idea.

'Well, Jameson informs me that it simply isn't the way things are done at Rosewater. According to him, the old ways are the best ways and "aren't no need to be changing up, Mister Gardiner, on account of some science nonsense". This is the attitude I am faced with, George.'

Sarah placed her hand on William's arm. 'George, I think it may be time for us to leave you. If William begins properly on this topic, we will be here until dawn. William?'

'My wife is a wise woman. Perhaps you could visit me at the mill some time, George, and I could show you what I mean.'

'Eliza,' Sarah said, 'thank you so much for your hospitality. Don't get up – William and I can find our own way out.'

Sarah kissed Eliza's cheek while the men shook hands, and then they were gone. A log tumbled in on itself in the grate.

'Why don't you go to bed, dear?' George said. 'I'll tidy up here.'

'Will you speak with Swanforth about the position?' She stayed seated, made no move towards bed.

They had all been talking about Swanforth, hadn't they? Something about Portland. About the lifeboat? No, about a daughter. What possible position could Eliza want him to assume with this daughter? He stared blankly at her and wondered if she had lost her mind.

'The position at the Sailors' Home, George. You remember?'

He nodded, though he certainly did not.

'Then you will speak with him? With the baby coming –' she patted her belly – 'it would be better for all of us if you were not so much at sea.'

'Of course. He's leaving soon, for Portland.' George knew that much. 'I should speak with him tomorrow.'

Eliza was satisfied. She packed away her cross-stitch, stroked his head and left the room.

Better for all of us if I was not so much at sea. Well, she might have something there, he thought. Perhaps a decent spell on dry land and the ocean-fed devils that haunted him would shrivel up, blow away. Perhaps he would learn to sleep and walk and think again like a human man.

George picked up the dishes scattered about the sitting room and dumped them on the kitchen table. He unwrapped the muslin from a cold roast leg of lamb in the pantry and carved a slice of the meat, then opened the kitchen door to the backyard and sat himself down upon the step.

He dangled the meat in front of him and whispered

the cat's name. He could hear her among the bushes in the neighbour's yard. There she was, leaping onto the wall. She ran towards him uttering tiny cries, tugged the meat from his hand and settled over it to eat. George ran a hand over the fur of her head and tried to share her joy.

Where had William been when he was cast out on that reef? Where had Sarah been when he had been alone and dying? No one had come for him.

Huddled on the wreck in those first hours, first days, of course, they had all said, they would be rescued soon. A passing ship, someone on shore: the alarm raised, the lifeboats sent, and then all of them home, warm and fed and dry. *We are they and they are we and soon they will be here to welcome us home.*

Those first days passed. Every morning fewer left – drowning, dying of thirst and exposure and despair, taken by sharks – and no one had come. Hour after hour after hour clinging to a submerged wreck in the middle of a freezing winter ocean. No food, no water. Hour after hour after hour after hour after hour after hour after hour. There had been no relief from the overwhelming feeling of terror for even a minute, even a second. And then suddenly, in one of those minutes, knowing that they would never come: that he had been abandoned to face this alone.

By the time the Portland lifeboat finally appeared, George had long since used up his last reserves of hope, optimism, compassion, and it had been some time since he could remember feeling even fear. He had been worn down to the bare nub of human consciousness. Those people on the lifeboat were no longer he; they were no longer we. The lifeboat appeared like a flimsy prop on a badly lit stage, came and left, came and left, and never saved a single one of them. Between each of its visits another handful would die. None of it mattered.

This was a new world he inhabited. He could not die, but would suffer on here for all eternity, visited by inhabitants of South Australia who would pull near in their boats to stare and to yell and then, as night fell, would return to their families and their homes and their sweet, rich existences. He would live here, always, in a world rimed in salt, his naked body chilled grey and swollen, his tongue cleaved forever to the roof of his mouth: the monstrous, undead king of Carpenters Reef. He had been abandoned. He was not human anymore; he was no longer a part of God's creation, but something outside it, undreamed of in God's all-seeing consciousness. He was a creature of the devil.

In the night, James Hare had died. He had been in life, in the world before Carpenters Reef, first steward of the ship. Now he was dead. He had somehow managed to pass on, to take the natural step of dying. He was gone now, in heaven, while George would live forever on the wreck of the *Admella*. It had been common practice, when a survivor sensibly died, to tumble their body off the sloping deck into the waves: for the dead, a burial at sea; for the ever-present sharks, a sacrificial meal. But at Hare's death it was though an unspoken agreement passed among those still left, an acknowledgment that this, now, was their life, that this wreck was their home and they no longer lived among humans or by human rules. Hare's body had been propped behind the stump of a mast to stop it rolling away, and the slumped shells of those who were left sat and stared upon it. It had been maybe minutes later, maybe hours, when the first of those whitened, swollen ghosts had dragged themselves across the deck to lie by Hare's body and to lick from his hair the dew that had accumulated during the night. George recalled sitting, watching, wrapped still in Miss Ledwith's arms, as one among them sucked the dead man's eyebrows, taking the moisture that was a ghost's right.

Had he torn the first shred of flesh, or was it another of his shipmates? He could not recall. All he remembered was the delicious feeling of wetness filling his parched, cracked mouth as he sucked the moist gobbet.

Whether or not he had been the first was irrelevant – there he was again, in his mind, prostrate before Hare's body, the familiar face beside his own, digging his nails into the skin to get purchase upon a lump of flesh.

Had he lain there for hours? Had it been mere minutes before the humans from the other world once more reappeared, yelling, throwing ropes, demanding attention from the ghosts who wanted nothing more now but to be left alone? He saw them from his wooden bed, watched them through his crusted eyes as they pulled closer and ever closer, calling once more about rescue, salvation. Soon they would go, like all the others had gone.

Only this time they did not. He turned his head and saw the captain, McEwan as he once was, clinging to a rope above the waves, making his way hand over hand into one of the noisy, insistent lifeboats. George turned his head once more, looked at the ghosts about him. Three were gone – were they in the water? Surely they were not in one of the boats? Of those who sat still, staring, everyone was perfectly quiet, and no person inclined to move.

George remained among them, his people. All this would pass. All this would pass. He slumped once more into Miss Ledwith's arms, felt again the crust of her skin against the flaking mess of his own. This was his home.

How had it come to pass that she had been taken from him? He could remember none of it but the feeling of being suddenly even colder, even more alone. He looked about himself and discovered that Miss Ledwith was gone. Bridget was gone. He had not realised he had any attachment to life left in him until that moment, when he felt it leave. He released his grip on the railings and rolled into the waves. But the waves, those instruments of the Lord, refused him. He tumbled instead into one of the infernal lifeboats, where the monstrous humans bent over him and declared that death was near. What did they know? Death was not for him. He lived now in another world.

He had woken in hospital, surrounded by humans, by light, by warmth, by noise. He was dry. He was warm. His skin was washed clean of salty crust. His tongue once more moved inside his mouth. He had been thrust back into humanity. He recalled the taste of Hare, and closed his eyes in horror. Had he really to live once more? How could such a thing be possible?

Why had the waves not taken him? Why was he here?

He pulled the cat to him but she struggled, evaded his grasp and disappeared into the night.

2

George had not married right away after his rescue, though that had been the plan. Eliza said she'd still be happy to have him, though he was broke and broken, but convention was on his side when he told her it was wrong to marry in such a state.

Instead, when they told him he wasn't about to die after all, George began searching for Miss Ledwith. He was not alone. All the papers wanted to find her, the only woman survivor of the terrible wreck. How had she lived through such horror? They speculated wildly on what she must have done, felt; where she could have got to. Perhaps she was a man, one said, in disguise. They sent a writer to Victoria, to the goldfields, and he sent word back that he'd met a young fellow, name of Trainor, who was probably Miss Ledwith, though they couldn't confirm it for certain. Chap had a certain tilt of the nose and a deathly terror of the ocean. The paper gave it eight hundred words. George would have liked to go see for himself, but with no money Victoria was out of the question.

She had not been a man in disguise. There was something bent about her, but that wasn't it.

George took work, went back to sea, made money. He kept his eyes open in port. If any woman passenger was shy, kept her face from view, he made extra sure to draw her out until he was certain that this woman was not her. As the months piled up, money piled up, George's arms and back and chest got stronger and his reasons for not marrying his fiancée began to look like what they were. For two months more he avoided Eliza and her family and their questions, telling himself he could have until April to solve this thing, to send her back to wherever it was she'd come from, to rid himself of her, and then he must knuckle down to a proper life. Two months.

There was an article in *The Argus*. An interview. She told the details of the famous wreck, apologised that she had needed time alone to recover but now she would return to live with her family in Morphett Vale. It was her. But the letter was as though she was a sensible human woman and that tilted George's conviction. She was a sea creature. He knew that. She had come into the boat from the ocean and she looked and smelled and felt all over like a human woman, but he was damn sure she was not.

George read the article in Melbourne and for the two days until they sailed he would not be stilled.

The ship docked in Port Adelaide. William was there, Eliza's sister's husband. He took George's arm and steered him to the pub and while George sat there fidgeting, thinking only about how he needed to set off, to find Miss Ledwith, sea creature or no, William lectured him on how he had put it off too long. It was time to marry Eliza or break off the engagement.

'Don't tell me,' William said, as George began explaining his ever-thinning reasons for delay. 'I'm not Eliza's messenger. You need to tell her yes or no. Tell her yourself.'

What was he supposed to say? *On the ship, William, on the wreck, I only stayed alive because this woman-not-woman wrapped me in her naked flesh. I don't know who or what she was. She said her name was Ledwith but I saw her with the horses and I can tell you she was no human woman generally and she was no Miss Ledwith specifically. Siren or whatever she was, she is why I am here now and I tell you I'm not ready yet to live life as though I am a normal living man. I ate human flesh, William, and I lived undead naked in this woman's arms. In all probability she is my unholy bride and how can I marry your sister-in-law, William, if that is the case? I have to find her and marry her or kill her or at least be convinced she is just a frail human woman and maybe then I can be the kind of casually human man that you are, drinking beer and talking about promises as though anything we do matters at all.*

But he said, 'I will, William. I have a small item of business to attend to and then I will visit Eliza and we will resolve this matter.'

William opened his mouth as if to say something more but for once he thought better of it. Instead, he took the paper he had tucked under his arm and passed it across the table to George. 'That young woman,' he said, 'the one from your ship. From the wreck. She's been writing to the paper.'

George stopped himself from stammering some kind of excuse, apology. William could not see inside his head, however smart the bloke thought himself. He breathed: once, twice. 'I saw,' he said, but then looked down at the paper and realised of course it was not *The Argus*, but *The Register*. 'Writing to *The Register*?' he said.

'Says there's an impostor about, some fraud claiming to be her in the Melbourne papers.'

'Oh.' George opened *The Register*, flicked to the letters page. 'It was with interest,' this woman wrote, 'that I read last week's *Argus*. That paper's article purported to be an interview with the only female survivor of the wreck of the *Admella*, a Miss Bridget Ledwith. Unpleasant as it may be, I must find fault with that esteemed journal, as I myself am the former Miss Ledwith.' It went on and on until 'Yours sincerely'. She signed, 'Mrs Ann Avage, Ballarat, Victoria'.

Ballarat? Mrs Ann Avage? He was not going to Ballarat to look for some woman who claimed to be married to a man called Avage. That was not going to happen. No succubus marries and changes her name to Avage; it simply doesn't happen.

'I will go see Eliza,' George said. 'Now. Why wait? I will go now.'

'Good man,' William told him.

3

After five hours of labour, Eliza had had enough and sent George to fetch the doctor. It was midafternoon, December, hot, and George felt his boots chafe and rub as he stomped down the streets of Port Adelaide. Dust blew up from the road and the grit of it got between his teeth.

At the door to the doctor's house, George rubbed his face with a handkerchief to remove some of the sweat and dirt, then rang the bell. The girl who worked there sat him down in the kitchen and poured him a glass of water, said wait.

'He can't come now,' she told George when she returned.

'Now is when we need him.' George kept most of the growl from the edge of his voice.

'Well, he isn't here. He's had to go to Largs for a lady, but I will send him on once he's back. Will you write your name and address?' She presented him with a piece of paper and a chewed pencil.

'Do you know how long he will be?' George laboured a little over the spelling of the street where they now lived, and instead just wrote *Seamens Home*.

'I couldn't say. But I'll have him to your wife as soon as possible. Would you like me also to send a message to the midwife in case she can come?'

'A midwife will do just as well. Better, even.' George wrote his name and address again and the girl said she would take the message herself, and that George should hurry home. 'Someone will be with you soon,' she told him. 'Tell your wife not to worry.'

Eliza did not look well, but George did not say so. While he was gone Sarah had arrived and was attending to her sister. She sent George from the room, told him to rest a while, that Eliza would be fine until the midwife arrived, or the doctor, should he come.

He would wait out the back. That way he would be handy if Sarah needed him, or to let the midwife in once she arrived. When would she arrive? He asked the cat, who lay stretched and rolling in a patch of sunny dust, rubbing the bugs from her fur. *Where is this wretched woman? Or this doctor, where is he?* George scratched his fingertips along the cat's belly and listened to her purr.

There was wood to be ordered for the stoves of the Sailors' Home. Butter too. A new latch for the stable door. George picked himself up off the back path and went inside, opened the account book, flicked back through the pages to see what Swanforth had paid last time and began writing out the orders. His ear wandered, listening for sounds from their quarters. Was that Eliza? Or that? He scribbled the numbers down and closed the book. She would live, of course she would. She was strong and young, healthy. No one healthier than Eliza. The whole thing had been going on far too long for his taste. Could the baby not just be born? He chewed at the end of the pen, scratched a picture on the blotting paper, an elephant standing on his hind legs and balancing a ball. Was that her? He leaned from the window to hear better, pulled his head back inside when he saw old Mitchell approaching up the road – that man loved nothing better than a mindless gossip and he would not talk now about his wife's condition.

He heard talking at the door: Sarah's voice and another woman's. His head went out again but they had retreated inside the house. Midwife – must be. He would write out the orders and that would take maybe ten minutes and then he would take his time walking by the bedroom. Just to check. He was within his rights to check, surely?

Butter. Stove wood. Latch. They were written. He sought out Stan Pieters, asked if he would be heading to the pub this afternoon, would he mind dropping off a few orders on his way? Pieters was only too happy, but did ask how the missus was doing, which George got held up answering.

Sarah heard him rattling the doorknob and slid herself out into the corridor before he could get a look at happenings on the bed.

'She's fine, George, leave her alone. The midwife is here. She's very experienced.'

'Will the baby come soon?'

'That's up to the baby, George.'

George went to look for the cat, but she wasn't coming for meat or threats. He cut down a tree because he could. In the end he walked down to the pub and bought himself a small whisky and a few more for luck. And it was as he was once again on his own doorstep wondering if he would ever be a father that he looked up and saw her, at the window, just once. It was her. There was a wave of sickness up from his belly and he left the whisky behind a bush in the yard. He righted himself and slammed the door open, stomped upstairs as fast as his slightly drunk-blurred boots would carry him, counted doors along the corridor to find the window she'd been at. The room was an empty one, perhaps to be filled when the family grew, for now just boxes and drop sheets. She wasn't under them and nor was she in them.

He heard a baby cry.

Was there a woman here? he wanted to yell at Sarah but listen, his baby had been born. He collected himself. He opened the door to their bedroom. Eliza was there and she was alive. Sarah was there too, watching Eliza, who was holding a tiny baby creature.

'The midwife?' he asked; he couldn't help himself.

'Gone half an hour since,' Sarah said.

'I mean,' he said, gathering his senses, 'she was paid?'

'She said she would call back for her money, as you were nowhere to be found. I'll make something for your dinner while you rest, Eliza.' Sarah kissed her sister's forehead and stroked a thumb across the baby's hair.

The woman would be back. George pulled up a chair beside his wife.

'Look, George,' Eliza said, and George ran a lightly exploring hand over the child's body, wondering in how many ways that woman had marked his boy.

'Henry?' he said.

'Of course,' she said. 'Henry Walter Hills. Your son.'

4

I am fleet-footed fur, feeding at the fingers of my first-known, my upright. This is a good life, sun on the belly in the morning. Feathers and fur all scampering about and me with my mouth full of their hot blood.

The other furry fleet-foots know me for what I am, hate me, but then they hate their own kind for the most part anyway. And from the uprights an occasional rock pitched at the head, a foot in the direction of my rump: small pains. The pleasures balance them. Find yourself a patch of fine gravel, stretch yourself as long as you'll go and onto your back roll, roll, roll: there isn't much finer unless it's to be flattened against the tickling grass one foot soft before the other, chin down low in that tickling grass, rump twitching and tasting already the wriggling between teeth, the wriggling below paw. They squirm so mightily!

But I have not come all this long way just to lose myself

in the wriggle of life against teeth. Universes die while I sleep stretched in the sun.

Where are my others? How did they fare? I leave my dusty bed behind and gather myself into seventeen more forms to search them out. In a crevasse under-ocean I see a flicker of familiar – eight writhing limbs and a coruscating skin. I am joy and all-over welcome but the creature flushes me with ink and flees. Nothing in its mind matches mine. We are siblings in shape only; I crush my hope and shift once more. I slide cold between stones and fly feathered to watch for my others from above but if we are still a proud race of warriors then we are being proud under a rock because I cannot find hide nor hair.

I cram myself once more into that upright form I'd held and take a turn about the rooms of my first-known's domain. But he comes stomping after me with fists all flailing so I take the chance to skitter small and claw-footed out of there. *Remember me,* I ask him, but if he hears me he doesn't say.

There is sun on my back but no one, no one to share it. The greatest adventure and no one to tell.

There is beauty and power and the throb of life but all of it is wrong: the wrong beauty, the wrong power.

These meagre joys of sun and dust are fine if you know no better but I had more, I had more. Sweet, yes, the momentary crunch of tiny bones and yes, how wonderful to be alive in the moment, yes? Yes. I want to be home. What is this place where some feeble race of uprights totter about the place in constricting rags, flailing their tentacles, and all other life stumbles quailing in their wake?

I watch my once-known and wonder in what world I end up wedged tiny in a crack in the wall trying to communicate with some foot-pounding menace whose brain is closed to anything that doesn't come in by eye, ear, mouth, nose or hand.

I am stuck here. There are no others of my kind. Day, night, day, night I have searched wet and dry and up and down and they are not here. Maybe they found a better place and no one ever sent for me. Maybe none survived. Maybe I am lost, confused; a wrong turn and I am in a dimension unexpected by any of us.

I squirm in my tiny furred form. There is too much dust here!

There is too much dust.

Upright has stomped elsewhere so I wriggle out. I pace on tiny feet the wooden floors of this place. Back; forth. My tiny heart pounds and aches. My tiny eyes see only to the corners of the room, not even strong enough to look outside. My tiny brain tries to remember how it felt to rule a world. I slip out under the door, scuttle down stairs, scamper myself into a room where a small one of this killer species is screaming its superior lungs out, biding its time before it, too, gets to roam about on its giant feet crushing bugs, ants, mice, hopes. This is your world, I tell it; yes, I know by now it will not hear me because nothing less than wavering sound will do for those fine ears, that fine mind. This is your world. Then I attach myself to its neck, its back; smooth and almost hidden, a birthmark that will never wash off. We are one now, I tell him, you will be my other. I dream him a dream of the endless sky, the hum of the stars. I dream him a world all ocean.

HENRY

1

'When you were wrecked,' Henry asked, 'what did you eat?'

'We didn't eat,' his father told him. 'There was nothing to eat.'

'Why didn't you eat the creatures in the sea?' Henry asked.

'What creatures? The fish? How would we have caught them?' His father took his hand and steered him through the traffic towards the crowd forming at the gates of the Glanville Estate. 'With our hands?'

'Yes, with your hands. You would have reached into the ocean and grasped them as they fled slippery by.'

'Henry, a man can't catch a fish with his bare hands. You need a rod or a reel – a hook at the very least. We had none of those.'

'The native man catches fish with his hands.' Henry felt sure it was true.

'Where do you learn these things, Henry? If he does, it

certainly isn't in the deepest ocean, waves towering over his head and crashing on his freezing skin. He'd be in a meadow, wouldn't he, lying happy in the sun and dandling his hands in a pleasant burbling brook. Grab himself out a trout or two, maybe. Are there trout here, Henry?' Henry's father ran his fingers tickling over Henry's chest and arms. 'Slippery little brook trout that a blackfella could catch with his hands?'

Henry didn't know about that. He couldn't quite remember why he'd asked.

'Have you seen this football before, Father?' he asked, squirming from the man's grip. 'Do you expect anyone will be hurt?' The butcher's apprentice, Mr Sidney, had told Henry he'd be playing today, that he meant to revenge some obscure crimes committed on him by various lads of the Port. Henry was keen to see it.

'It may happen. Perhaps a man will fall and hurt his head or his leg. Slow down, Henry!' But Henry dodged between horses, carts and a crowd of gents on foot and didn't care whether George could follow.

The game had already begun when they found a spot on the field where they could see the action, such as it was. The crowd milled about, following the ball as it tumbled and bounced first one way, then back the other, the players sprinting after it and trying to bring it under control.

'Do you know which men are Port?' Henry's father asked a man standing beside him.

'In the blue and white,' the man told him.

'Is there a score yet?'

'No score yet, sir.'

'Not surprising,' he told the man. 'Even the players don't seem to know which way they should head to the goal.'

Henry was staring into a pile of men, where, deep in its midst, he could see one had another's private-most parts gripped in his fist. The gripped man wriggled and tried to flee but the fist was too tight.

'Show them, Port!' Henry muttered. 'Beat those Young Australians!'

Overhearing the boy, George asked, 'Henry, shall we go up to the house and find some lemonade?'

'Oh, not now. I think Port will be champions!'

As it turned out, though, they were not. After some hours of play, the score was still nil all and, as the sun had gone down, the spectators began to disperse.

On the walk home, an hour or more, Henry watched his thoughts play about behind his eyes. His father, sat enthroned on a pointed jumble of wreck, watching as silver bodies sped past just out of reach. All around him, the purple-white faces of his shipmates scanning the waves for help. Sharks, leaping, teeth flashing sunlight. An arm torn from its socket and a spout of blood shooting for the sky.

Mother had left them tea on the kitchen table and Father took his away to his office. Little Georgie, Wills, the new baby, and Mother had all gone to bed. Henry would sleep soon too but for now he sat chewing on a pie crust, swinging his feet. He had wanted to ask Father if they could get a cat to keep, but he had forgotten. There were cats everywhere – they prowled the stable out back, living on rats and mice – but Henry would have liked one that was mostly his. Cats were never really anyone's, he knew that, but it would be nice to have one that was mostly his. Henry slipped his hand inside the collar of his shirt and stroked at the edges of his Mark, using just the tips of his fingers. He would feed the cat scraps and it could come with him on his walks around the neighbourhood. Sometimes it would sleep in the cupboard under the back stairs, where Henry kept his experiments. Henry picked some pieces of sausage meat from his pie and held them to his shoulder so his Mark could eat, then he washed the crumbs from his mouth with the last dregs of his milk and went upstairs to bed.

2

Beatrice Gallwey had come to South Australia from the colony of New South Wales. Her husband had died, the way husbands so often do. A bite from a flea or a mosquito, they said, and some infection of the blood. It hadn't taken terrifically long. They didn't like each other much, Bea and her husband, and she didn't miss him but still, she'd rather they'd got around to leaving one another than that he was cold in the ground. She wouldn't have held it against him had he found somewhere else to go.

That left Bea and the daughter. She hadn't paid Meredith all that much attention for most of her life. She appeared to be well-behaved if a little grim. So it had come as quite a surprise to discover that a year after her father's death and not that long since her seventeenth birthday, the girl was planning to have some fellow's child.

The man meant to marry her, Merri told Bea when she

asked. 'Well, that's good, I suppose,' Bea had said, assuming that was generally the way things went. No point kicking up a fuss now, the deed's done, the kid's on the way. 'I suppose he'll have a way to look after you?' she'd asked. 'This husband?' Merri supposed he would – he had a business fixing shoes and pans, sharpening knives. 'So he's a gypsy then,' Bea had suggested, and Merri had been outraged though she'd meant nothing by it other than to establish whether the chap was, in fact, a gypsy.

It turned out the chap was a gypsy, which Beatrice confirmed on meeting the man and his family at the wedding. It was a nice wedding and Bea had been happy to help pay for it, happy to see her daughter less grim, happy to see her with someone to care for and to care for her now her father was gone. The dancing had been fevered. Bea hadn't minded at all, had danced with gusto. A brother of someone's wife had joined her and when he'd left her bed the next morning she had been sorry to see him go.

The baby came along, born safe and happy and the mother safe and happy too. They'd named him Ivan, which Bea thought a little extravagant, but kept his middle name as Edward in honour of the child's maternal grandfather. Bea had been thinking about moving somewhere a little smaller, now it was just her. Maybe to the country. Cessnock sounded lovely, and enough people there to keep her in work. She'd begun selling off some of her heavier belongings, the leather armchair her husband had fawned over and the hundred or so books he'd read and re-read while sitting in it. His writing desk. His mother's silver tea set. His gold watch she put away for Ivan, and Merri had insisted on keeping Daddy's set of ivory and ebony pens. Bea gave some of the money to Merri and the rest she put aside in preparation for the move.

Merri showed up on the doorstep mid one Sunday morning. Bea had been giving her viola a going-over and didn't hear the door for a while. By the time she did, Merri was a little red-faced and glowering, which was nothing Bea wasn't used to.

'Come in,' she told the girl, who was carrying little Ivan all wrapped up in a blanket far too warm for the weather. A small suitcase sat forebodingly at her feet. Merri didn't come in.

'Going somewhere?' Bea asked, noticing the husband's cart across the street, packed to the brim with household goods.

'We're going up the Hawkesbury,' Merri told her. 'Michael' – the husband – 'has had enough of Sydney. He says we need some space around us.'

'The Hawkesbury? I've been thinking of moving to Cessnock myself.'

Merri dismissed this with a sceptical eyebrow. 'Yes, but we really are going. We're going now.'

'Yes, I can see that.' Bea wondered if the whole family

was going, or just these three. 'Well, let me know where you settle, if you settle. It would be good to know where you are.'

Merri looked impatient. 'Yes, Mother.'

'And I'll leave my details with the postmaster here, should I ever actually stir myself to leave town. So you can find me, should you need to. Now, do you need anything else of your father's? I intend to sell the lot of it. Oh, I should at least give you his watch, for Ivan. Wait,' she said, 'and I'll fetch it.'

'Mother, there's no need. I want Ivan to stay with you.' She held the baby out. 'Take him, please.'

'I don't want your baby, Merri. What do I want with a baby?'

'Well, I don't want him either. He cries all the time. He doesn't sleep, he doesn't want my milk. I'm sick of him. Michael's sick of him too. We have things to do. We want to travel. What?' Merri glared at her mother.

'You could take him to the orphanage,' Bea suggested.

'Don't be ridiculous! He doesn't belong in an orphanage, he has a perfectly good family. I'll come back for him later,' Merri said. 'When he's bigger. When he doesn't cry so much and I don't have to watch over him every single second of the day. Just take him!'

Beatrice folded her arms and stared at her daughter. Merri responded by putting the baby down on the doorstep and walking off. Michael waved from the cart and then they were gone.

Bea tried not to let the fact of a baby in the house get too much in the way of her plans. But she had to admit, it made it much more difficult for her to go out to work. One of the places where she did a little cleaning didn't mind so much if she left the baby in the laundry while she worked; the others were set against it. It was as though she had no moral right, a woman her age and with a husband well and truly dead, to have a baby with her. She explained the situation but the feeling about the place was that she was clearly in the wrong.

Merri never did send word where she'd gone – no surprises there. Bea wondered if she could offload the kid to her sister, who had a fondness for family that Bea couldn't claim. The sister, Anne-Marie, had set sail for Port Adelaide seven years back, and once or twice a year Bea got a letter from Burnside, where the family had settled, extolling the virtues of the colony and now and again suggesting Beatrice and her husband make the move. It would be lovely to see you, Anne-Marie always claimed. *Then lovely it shall be,* thought Beatrice. *Why not South Australia? There's nothing keeping me here in St Peters. I'm sure Burnside has just as much to offer as Cessnock. Perhaps I could pick grapes.*

So Beatrice sold off the rest of the furniture and booked a passage for herself and Ivan to Port Adelaide. She told the postmaster she was leaving, on the off chance Merri ever came looking for her boy, with the promise she would send more details once she was settled. And she wrote ahead to

Anne-Marie to let her know she was coming. Ivan did not get a mention.

They arrived in the new colony on a perfectly horrid day, cold wind and a putrid spitting rain that made Bea want to get back on the boat and go home to the soft warmth of New South Wales. Instead she found a hotel that would take her and the boy for a night. She washed them both and changed their clothes, then set out to find the post office to see if Anne-Marie had replied to her letter.

'Scarlet fever,' the letter said. 'Better not to come now. We have all been very ill. It would not be safe.'

They had a poor night's sleep, men downstairs in the public bar yelling till all hours, and Bea wondered if that kind of thing was legal here in South Australia, and of course as soon as they stopped the baby started up. Some kind of breakfast and Bea, determined to see for herself how things stood, found someone who would take them to Burnside. Their seachest stayed behind.

No one answered the door of her sister's house but a neighbour, seeing her there, asked if she had come far. 'From Sydney,' Beatrice said, and that was enough to earn her a cup of tea and as much information as she wanted. Her sister's husband and one of the children had died. Anne-Marie had taken the other children to live with the husband's family in Hahndorf, perhaps two weeks ago. The neighbour couldn't say for sure whether the arrangement was permanent but a woman with five children to raise, well, it was unlikely she'd be back here trying to fend for herself. Beatrice, with her one feeble hanger-on, was inclined to agree. The neighbour had a cousin in the Port, though, ran a boarding house and could probably help with finding Beatrice a position, if she decided she'd stay. The weather was less revolting today and so Beatrice thought she might as well. She took the cousin's name and address and a letter of introduction and wondered what a woman would have to do to get a drink around these parts.

No one likes a screaming baby in a boarding house. Working men are particularly against the whole idea. That situation lasted three weeks before Bea found a woman, single like her, willing to rent out the unused stable at the back of her place for a measly sum, with use of the house's kitchen and a place where she could wash. It was a step down in the world from her pleasant little villa in St Peters, but Beatrice liked the strangeness of it. No one bothered her there. No one asked stupid questions about the child or where her husband or her daughter had got to. Her landlord was happy to send the houseboy now and again to buy a bottle of gin they could share, and on warmer evenings – it turned out Port Adelaide had many warm evenings, much pleasanter than Sydney after all – the three of them would spend a civilised hour or two on a couple of upturned crates in the paved area between the stable and the house, sipping their drinks and musing on the funny ways life has about it. Sometimes Bea would get out her viola and the boy had his flute and they'd have a bit of a sing. Otherwise, Bea was left to her own devices. Ivan got used to sleeping in a drawer and eventually started tottering about on his own two feet and making up nonsense words, and the houseboy was happy to watch the kid when Bea needed to go out to work. If all family life was like this, Bea thought, perhaps she would have been a better mother and wife.

3

When Henry was small, Mother told him, she had sometimes worried about his birthmark. She'd scrubbed at it to wash it off, but it hadn't gone. She'd even taken him to the doctor once, but the doctor had said of course it was nothing to worry about. And that's what she told him, too: that it was nothing to worry about. He'd asked, when he was three, who his Mark was and Mother had told him not who but what, that Mark was part of his skin, that Mark was Henry. But Mark gets so hungry, he told Mother, and sometimes even when I'm not hungry. And Mark likes fish and I don't like fish. And Mother had kissed him and told him to stop being silly, not to talk like that, and so from then on he never had.

Anyway, they had always been together. And Mark was his business, no one else's. Whenever father saw Mark he always told Henry, 'Put on a shirt,' though he never said why.

Mark told him things no one else knew. When Henry talked about those things Mother told him to change the subject but other people either stared or laughed or sometimes they got angry. Father got angry. At first Henry hadn't realised he was the only one who knew about these things. He'd wanted to talk to other people about the world that was entirely ocean, about the taste of skin felt through your tentacles and why his tentacles could never taste a thing. Henry had seen into space. Henry knew how it was to catch a live and slippery thing between your teeth. But no one else knew about these things and so Henry stopped asking. Sometimes Henry would pretend that the things he knew were just things he'd thought, imagined, wondered, and then he could tell them to Uncle William and Uncle William would tell him things back. Sometimes Aunty Sarah would help him draw pictures of the things inside his head. Today they were drawing what might happen if you were a human and you tried to live under the ocean.

'What would you drink?' Henry asked. 'How would you breathe?'

'Well, I think humans need air to breathe,' Sarah began.

'How do fish breathe, then?'

Sarah drew him a quick picture of a fish and showed him the place on the side of their heads where they have long holes, covered by flaps of skin. 'These are their gills,' she said. 'Fish pull water inside them through the gills and then they suck all the air out of the water to breathe it, then they push the water back out.'

'There's air in water?'

'There's air in the water. Think of the bubbles in the bath – they're full of air.'

Henry thought about them. 'So humans could build a city under the water if they could learn how to get the air out of the water?'

'I suppose so. Perhaps they'd use a machine. Do you want to draw a machine? I suppose it would have to be small so the human could carry it around with him.'

Henry drew what he thought that would look like, and Sarah did too. Henry's machine was on a little wheeled cart and the air went from a tube right through the human's chest and into his lungs. Sarah had drawn a machine that looked like a knapsack, and a breathing mask the human could wear over his mouth.

'Can humans drink salt water?' Henry asked. 'Isn't the water in the ocean salty?'

'The water in the ocean is definitely salty,' Sarah told him. 'I'm pretty sure we can't drink it – I think it makes us sick and maybe even kills us, though I'm not sure why.'

'Then how would people drink under the ocean? What do fish drink? Can fish drink salt water?'

'I don't know if fish need to drink,' she said. 'Maybe because they're in the water all the time they don't ever need to drink it.'

'But humans would need to. What do humans do when they're out on ships for a very long time? What do they drink then?'

'They have to take barrels of water with them. If they run out, they're in trouble.'

'You should ask your father,' Uncle William butted in. He'd been reading, ignoring Henry's questions all afternoon. 'He'd know. They had no water on the wreck, he says. Nothing to drink for days and days. Seems impossible to me, but that's how he tells it.'

'Shut up, William,' Sarah said. 'Don't ask your father, Henry. We can figure it out ourselves.'

But Henry already knew it was true they had had nothing to drink when they were stuck on the wreck. His Mark had shown him; he'd seen it over and over. Sometimes Father would talk to him about it but sometimes he got angry and told Henry to leave him the hell alone, but Henry was never sure which it would be.

'I have an idea,' Henry said, and he drew a human under the water with a tube that went up to a tank, floating on the ocean's surface. 'Every time it rains,' he explained, 'the tank fills up with fresh water and the human can take a drink from the tube. There's a plug in the end of the tube under the ocean but anyone who's passing by can pull the plug out and take a drink.'

'Perfect!' said Sarah. 'A perfect solution.'

'Probably what saved them on the *Admella*,' William said.

'If you're not reading,' Sarah told him, 'why don't you come and help? We're trying to draw all the animals in the sea. Sharks we know about, right?' Henry nodded vigorously. He was particularly good at drawing sharks.

'And of course there are all the eating fish, mulloway and mackerel and John Dory.'

'How many fish do you think there might be in the sea?' Henry asked.

'An uncountable mass,' William said. 'Beyond imagining.'

'Hmm. It is quite something to think on,' said Sarah. 'It was a busy day for God when he created the creatures that swim in the waters, I expect.'

'That is one way to see things.' William found his bookmark and closed the volume he was reading, put it down on the table beside his armchair. 'On the other hand,' he continued, 'it is enlightening to think that all those fish came from a single species which diversified and diversified, changing to match its circumstances, over millions and millions of years.'

'I'm not sure which idea I find more fanciful, or more delightful,' said Sarah. 'Both have their charms. I think I shall suspend judgement for now.'

'Did we come from fish?' Henry asked. 'Did we used to live under the water?'

'You and I?' said William.

'Yes. You and I and all the other humans. All the animals. Were we all fish once? Were all animals fish?'

'Well, now, let's see,' said William. 'If one goes back far enough, the ancestor of you and me was an ape, like a chimpanzee. But that chimpanzee must also have had ancestors, I suppose – some simpler kind of mammal, perhaps like mice. And those mice must have come from somewhere, though I can't say for sure where.' William stood up from his chair and began searching the bookshelves. 'Ah, yes, here.' He flicked through the pages then placed the book open on the table where Henry and Sarah were drawing. 'Now here is what scientists are calling a tree of life. And let's see.' Henry's eyes scoured the diagram, trying to understand what it all meant, and he could feel his Mark pushing him to try harder, think harder, learn harder. William pointed to the picture. 'Here at the top, that's us: MAN. And as you see if you follow that trunk down, you soon get to apes, then semi-apes, then primitive mammals, which is the point where we join all our furry warm-blooded friends. You see, Henry? If you trace our ancestry back this far, that is where we become one with the horses and the sheep and the tigers. Now follow the tree down … Well, yes, if we do keep going down it seems that although life began as amoebae – little creatures so tiny we can't even see them, Henry – before long it was turning into crustaceans and molluscs and primitive fishes.'

Henry stretched out his arm to touch the page, ran his

finger over the drawings of molluscs – the nautilus, the octopus.

William carried on. 'It does appear the primitive fishes became the amphibians who became the primitive mammals who became the apes who became us. So yes, Henry, I guess we did all come from fishes.'

Sarah was leaning over Henry, trying to get a good look at the diagram. 'What are the whales doing all the way over here with the horses and the sloths? Shouldn't they be down the bottom with the fishes?'

'Hmm.' William stared closer. 'Well, that is perplexing. A transcription error, perhaps,' he said, and closed the book.

Henry reached to grab it from him. 'No, wait!' he said. 'Show me again!'

William opened the book.

'These are the creatures,' Henry murmured. 'Soft and shifting. With strong tentacles and suckers that grip.' He stroked the pictures again, felt a sad, grasping kind of comfort seeping from the Mark on his back.

'The molluscs?' William said. 'A kind of soft animal, a creature without bones. You know the only hard part of its whole body is the beak it uses to eat? A very early animal, Henry. No one really knows where they came from.'

'Older even than the fishes?'

'That's right. Because fishes couldn't exist until bones were invented, and it took a long time to evolve bones. Your creatures got a head start because they decided bones weren't necessary to their development. They could get on just fine without them.'

'So maybe that's where we all came from?'

'No, it doesn't quite work like that. We all came from the soft worm that turned into the first fish, you see?' William ran his finger over the diagram.

Henry nodded. 'And once, everyone that was lived under the water. Once the whole earth was ocean.'

'Well, not technically, Henry. There was still land, plenty of land, it was just that nobody lived on it.'

'How strange,' Sarah said. 'In a sense, then, the whole world was ocean.'

'Yes, in a sense,' William agreed.

'What a thing to think about,' she said. 'I really never have before. That all the life on this earth lived in the ocean. Everyone there was, was a fish.'

'Or a soft worm or some other kind of mollusc. A sea squirt or maybe a starfish. Perhaps some kind of sponge,' William went on.

'And *we* once were fish,' said Henry. 'Once we could live under the ocean too, and breathe the water and drink the water. And then we changed, and we had to come out onto the land or we would have drowned or died of thirst. And then we couldn't float anymore and we had to learn how to stand up and walk around, which was a lot harder. And when we were standing up we got embarrassed because everyone could see us, and we invented clothes. And now we wish that maybe we could go back under the water and live and breathe and drink there, and just float all the time and never wear clothes. We could be fish again.'

He reached for a fresh piece of paper and began to draw. He drew his mother and his father and Georgie and little Wills, and he drew Sarah and William, and none of them were wearing clothes and they were all shaped as though they had no bones, just floating about. He added tentacles here and there, and gills on the sides of their heads. Around them coloured fish were swimming and sharks and there were starfish and four tentacled creatures. Up in the top corner a boneless tiger was swimming after a boneless sheep.

Across the bottom he wrote ALL ONE ANIMUL IN THE UNDER WATER WURLD.

'Everyone lives together,' he told Sarah, 'and each animal has a home to live in and a type of thing it is all right for them to eat. They shouldn't eat other things – that would be unfriendly. And they each just do that and don't try to be different or to run things. Even the humans. See? The humans swim about and eat the creatures they're allowed to eat and they don't kill anyone else they shouldn't. They stay in their niche. The tiger eats the sheep but it doesn't eat the shark.'

'Their what, Henry?'

'Their niche. They stay in it.' Henry dropped the pencil he had been clutching. 'Are there any more biscuits, please? I feel very hungry now.'

'Yes, I think a biscuit might be a good idea. And a cup of tea? Dear, tea for you? William?'

William was staring fixedly at Henry's drawing.

'Pardon? What?'

'You should have a cup of tea, William.'

'I should? Oh, yes. A cup of tea, thank you. That would be lovely. Henry, this is a marvellous drawing – do you think I could keep it?'

'Oh yes, good idea, Uncle William. Could we keep it, Henry?' Sarah asked.

Henry picked the picture up off the table by its corner and stared at it. He shrugged, and passed the picture to his aunt. She slid it between the pages of Haeckel's guide and put the book back on the shelf, tapped its spine a couple of times as though to make sure everything was safe and locked away. Then she went into the kitchen.

'So you like sea creatures, Henry?' William asked.

But Henry was sick of thinking about being under the ocean and what it might be like to be always wet and to breathe water. He wanted to live here for a moment. It was warm here. Being dry was actually rather nice.

'Uncle William,' he asked, 'can you die from drinking flowers mixed with water?'

Uncle William rubbed his hand over his eyes and sat back down in his armchair.

'I guess what I mean really is,' Henry continued, 'is there a way to find out if flowers in water could kill you without actually dying?'

'What kind of flowers are they, Henry?'

'White.'

'Oh, Sarah, tea! Thank you, just the ticket! Now, your Aunty Sarah has been working on a new recipe for apple cake, haven't you, Sarah? Maybe she'd like to try making one? Maybe you could help her? What do you think, Henry?'

'Would you like to make a cake with me?' Sarah asked.

'When it's made will we eat it?' Henry asked.

'Yes, of course.'

'Aunty Sarah,' he said, as they went into the kitchen. 'Did you know that old Missus Gallwey who lives in the stable behind us has a baby in a box in the attic?'

'I didn't know there was an attic in the stable,' she said. 'That's very interesting. She isn't really that old, though. Maybe only ten years older than I am.'

'She's a grandma. The baby is her grandson.'

'Well, I suppose she is very old then. Now, do you want to peel the apples for me? Perhaps you'd like to take some cake to Missus Gallwey and her grandson once we're done.'

'I'm not allowed to play with her, she's a washerwoman and a reprobate and maybe even a witch,' Henry said.

'Though I don't suppose giving someone cake is playing.' He arranged the apples in a pyramid on the bench, then took the top one from the pile and started peeling it with the lovely sharp little knife Sarah had given him. 'Look,' he told her, 'your lovely sharp little knife can make one very, very, very, very long piece of apple peel.'

'Oh, that might be as much the work of my lovely sharp little nephew,' she said, perplexingly, and kissed the top of his head.

4

Three children. A happy wife – happy enough. Work. A home to live in, money enough to live on. Legs that walked, arms that lifted, eyes to see and teeth to chew. Everything in order, tiptop, shipshape.

Black anger, black dread and a heart that stopped, stopped, stopped then started again. Lungs made of tin, wouldn't stretch to let the air in. And trying to walk around like a man with children, a happy wife, work, a home to live in and all the rest of it. Smile like a man. Laugh like a man. Drink like a man. Work like a man. But this thing inside was something else.

'Go to the doctor,' Eliza had said, when she'd found him that day slumped on the front doorstep trying to breathe like he'd run in terror from some ancient monster reared dripping from the sea. There had been no ancient monster. He hadn't even run. He was standing and then he was passing out and then he'd come back to his senses with the grip of terror still on his heart. The dead smoke of some monster still in his nostrils and behind his eyes. 'It could be your heart,' she'd said. 'Please, see the doctor.'

If it was his heart, what could the doctor do except tell him he was doomed and to take to his bed? There was no fixing a busted heart. Worse, the doctor would open him up and tell him, 'Sir, there's nothing in you but oily muck, just a stinking green paste I don't know what it is, I've never seen the like of it, sir.' They'd prop him up in some doctors' museum and they'd all poke at him. 'Look at him,' they'd say, 'a man but not a man, how is he even alive when he has nothing inside but muck?'

So he went to the doctor. 'Could there be something the matter with my heart, Doctor? With my lungs?' He asked with the voice of a man with a family, responsibilities. 'I cannot leave my wife and three children, Doctor. Can you tell me what's wrong and then can you fix me?'

The physician was unnervingly young. His dark curly hair extended into sideburns that expanded across his face in mutton-chops. As he peered into George's eyes, George noticed that his lips were somewhat too moist, but that his nostrils seemed uncommonly clean.

'Turn around, please, sir.'

The doctor tapped on his back, then listened to it with some instrument.

'Is there anything there, Doctor?'

'Please be quiet, sir. I need you to be quiet.'

He breathed quietly and shallowly.

'If you could please breathe a little deeper, sir.'

The air shuddered into George's lungs, and back out again.

'All right, thank you. Please put your shirt back on, sir.'

George tugged the shirt over his head and stood up to tuck it in. The mirror stared back at him, showing his grey hairs, his yellowing eyes. Death was all over him.

'Have you any idea what it is, Doctor?' he asked.

'Mister Hills, I have never felt more confident in saying that there is absolutely nothing wrong with you, sir. A fitter and healthier man I have rarely seen. Now –' he looked at his notes – 'you say you suffered some physical trauma in the past?'

'Yes, I was on a shipwreck. The doctor then, the one who looked me over when they rescued me, he said that I would not live. My organs were smashed, something inside – the main mast of the boat fell on me. I was beaten badly from being thrashed about in the ocean, too. We couldn't drink or eat. It was … it wasn't so good out there. Rough on the body.'

'And –' the doctor looked at his notes – 'you have a broken thumb. From the same event?'

George nodded. Thumb? Who cared about his thumb?

'But you did live, despite that diagnosis, and I have to say that aside from some scarring, you appear to have suffered no long-term effects from your ordeal. How long were you without food and water?'

'Eight days.'

'Eight days? The doctor was right – you should be dead. You are clearly a man of substantial constitution.'

'So what's the matter with me? My heart is weak?'

'Your heart is in no way weak.'

'And my lungs? Is it pneumonia? Consumption.'

'There is nothing. Your breathing is better than one could expect for a man your age.'

A man my age, he thought. *I could beat you within an inch of your life, a man my age, you scoundrel.* 'There is nothing?'

'Nothing at all. There is nothing wrong with you.'

George did not want to ask but he was here now and so he may as well find out the worst of it. 'Then why does my heart stop beating for no reason at all, Doctor? Why can I not draw breath in my lungs if I am such a strong, healthy man?'

'It could be …' The doctor looked uncomfortable, tapped with his pencil on the wood of his desk.

'What? Is it a tumour?'

'It could be your mind has become unsettled. There are things we are only just beginning to understand about how thoughts in the mind may disturb the functioning of the body …'

'Are you saying I'm imagining it? That I'm imagining my lungs can't breathe?'

'No, sir, no – not at all. It's more that it's possible there can be things hidden deep in our minds that, well, display themselves as physical symptoms …'

'Insanity. You're saying I'm losing my mind.'

'It isn't that. But if you like I can refer you to a very reputable hypnotist who may …'

'Thank you, no.' He would not have some crank delving about in the workings of his head. They would lock him up as soon as look at him once they found the greasy muck he had hidden inside. No, he would solve this thing himself. 'No. Thank you, Doctor. If there is nothing wrong with me then there is nothing wrong with me. Whatever it is will surely pass. Good day.'

She was walking around out there in Ballarat or Morphett Vale or wherever the hell it was she'd ended up, living off the thing inside him that had made him human. And now his heart didn't work like a heart should work and his lungs were flaps of useless paper in his chest and even his mind had turned on him, was telling him there was something behind him, something behind him, always something behind him and there never was.

She had been in his house. He had seen her, that day: the day Henry was born. She had been in his house and she had touched his wife and his boy and God only knows what she had done to them. When he couldn't find her, when she never returned for the money but sent another woman in her stead – oh, Sarah said of course this was the same woman, 'What are you talking about, George?', but it wasn't, it wasn't, she had pulled the wool over all their eyes – he had tried to tell himself it had been his mind playing tricks. A trick of light, of shadow, that he had seen her face up there in that upstairs window. But she had been there in the room that now was Henry's room, Georgie's room. What had she left in there? How might she have touched his boys?

She had been in his house. He had let eight years pass, had let himself be fobbed off with comforting thoughts that it was his imagination, that another woman had been the midwife. He had let himself believe that Henry had escaped unscathed but he knew it wasn't true. That thing on his back, the oddness of his mind. George needed to stand up, be a man, take responsibility. The time for comfort was passed. Not another minute.

He stormed into the Sailors' Home, heard Wills crying and Eliza trying to hush him, heard Henry and Georgie chasing one another up and down the stairs and called to them to keep quiet, let the baby sleep. He ignored Pieters, who was asking if he'd heard back yet from the new woman who was meant to be coming to clean, and went into his office and locked the door. He pulled all the papers from the bottom drawer in his desk – they were a terrible mess, just pile upon pile – and dumped them on the floor, spread them in a circle about him. Not that, not that, not that: this. And this. The two letters from the alleged Bridget Ledwiths. Of course he had hung on to them. Of course he had slid them into the bottom drawer of his desk when they moved here to the Sailors' Home. He had known he would need them again one day.

'Dear Miss Ledwith,' he wrote, then stopped. He had been about to write, 'It is George Hills who lay by you for eight days and nights on the wreck of the *Admella*. You have destroyed me. I need you to give me back what is mine.' But of course that wouldn't do. Only one of these women was Ledwith. It was possible neither of these women was Ledwith. And what would a woman think, who wasn't Ledwith, on reading such a thing? She would call the police and the police would come and they would lock him up in an asylum.

'Dear Miss Ledwith,' he wrote, 'It has been many long years since we last saw one another but I trust you will still remember me. My name is George Hills, and I was a cabin steward on the steamship *Admella*. I am sorry to remind you of that unfortunate incident and I hope that thinking upon it does not cause you too much discomfort. However, I hope that you may be prepared to correspond with me. I know you have taken pains to keep your privacy since that event, and if you choose to reply to my letter I will certainly respect that wish. Since the wreck I have found certain difficulties and physical symptoms have arisen for me. Doctors have been unable to help. I merely wish to speak with someone whose experiences match my own and who may be able to shed some light on whether there is a connection between that unpleasant incident and my current state of ill health. If you would not mind corresponding with me, you may reach me at the address above. Otherwise, I wish you all the best. Yours sincerely, George Hills.'

He then wrote the letter again, this time addressed to Mrs Avage.

When Henry got home, carrying some kind of cake, he told the boy to go down to the post office and have them sent. He saw Henry walk out the front door, still carrying part of the cake, and head off with the letters tucked in his pocket.

It was done.

Neither of those women was likely to be her. Neither of them was her: he already knew. They were too – what was the word? – quotidian. He would take out an advertisement, place it in the papers in South Australia, Victoria and New South Wales. Surely she wouldn't have gone further than that.

He sat back at his desk.

Are you Miss Bridget Ledwith? Were you ever her? I am not a newspaperman or a detective. I was on the ship. I have something of yours. Please get in contact.

Are you or do you know Miss Bridget Ledwith? I need to find her urgently.

Are you Bridget Ledwith? I know secrets about you. Write to me at this address and I will never tell.

Spirit woman, you were on the Admella *when she went down. I know you were not what you seem. Write to me at this address so I can sleep at night and breathe like a normal man.*

The last, that was the right one. Only she would know what he meant. He wrote it neatly, clearly. He could not give this to Henry to do. He could not do it from the telegraph office here. He would have to travel to the city, where he was not known. His piles of paper back into the bottom drawer; the advertisement, the ink dry now, slid between the pages of this morning's *Register*.

'I'm going into Adelaide,' he called to no one in particular, but Pieters heard and asked, again, whether the new cleaning woman would be coming today. George put the newspaper down but kept one hand on top of it as he searched through the Home's journal.

'Tomorrow, she'll be here tomorrow. Anything else?'

There wasn't. He stuck his head in to his own kitchen and asked loudly whether anyone needed anything in Adelaide, but as no one replied he felt he had done his duty.

As he settled into his seat on the Adelaide train, George suddenly remembered his childhood dream of being a duck herder. Aged eight, he'd been, back in Chigwell: he'd told the old man he wanted to grow up to farm ducks. That'd be the life, herding his flock of ducks about the countryside from pond to creek and back again, sitting in the shade of a tree and watching his flock splashing in the water, eating a Scotch egg and drinking a mug of porter. An eternal English summer, forget the damp and wind and snow he would face half the year, the death of ducks taken by foxes and all the other unpleasantness that would go along with such a life. You couldn't do it here, though, could you, where not foxes but dingos would prey on the ducks and summers would be spent desperately seeking out water for the flock. Did men even farm ducks in South Australia? He had no idea, he realised, and could not in fact pinpoint the last time he had seen a duck.

5

Henry was bored.

He had cleaned his room.

He had helped Mother bring in the firewood.

He had fetched down the winter coats from the attic – found Georgie curled up among them, pretending to be a bear – and then hung them outside to air.

He had sat with Wills on Mother and Father's bed and tried to teach the baby to bark, but Wills had just giggled at him and, after a while, cried.

He had talked to each and every last sailor in the home. He had interviewed them one by one, asked whether they had ever been bitten by a shark or seen someone else eaten by one, or if they had met a pirate or even been a pirate once upon a time. One man said he had seen his shipmate fall overboard and be eaten by a shark, and Henry had asked him if he could please give some more detail, like exactly how big was the shark and how many bites did it take to eat the man and did the man make any interesting faces while he was being eaten, or did the shark start with his face. And he had stood there with his pencil and his paper ready to write whatever the sailor said, but the sailor had said he couldn't remember all that much of it, that he had turned away almost as soon as the shark appeared. And Henry closed his book of paper and put his pencil back in his pocket and wondered why a person would turn away when they could watch a shark eating a man. How often does a person get a chance to have an experience like that?

Henry had eaten a bun.

He had eaten a handful of grapes from the bunch he'd been told not to touch.

He had gone out the back to the apple tree he was not supposed to climb and he had climbed the tree and got one of the very best apples from the top and sat there eating it until all that was left was the core.

Henry had added the core to his experiment shelf. The shelf was in the cupboard under the back staircase where nobody else ever went. It was the seventeenth core on the shelf, and the first and second ones had some quite lovely worms living on them. Next to them was the rat that one of the home's cats had caught – its tail was missing and its eyes, but so far he couldn't see any of the rest of its skeleton.

He shook his jar of scabs. It was still only about a quarter full. He thought about grazing Georgie's knees and ankles and adding Georgie's scabs. That could ruin the experiment. He didn't know what the experiment was, so he wasn't sure.

Henry sat for a while and stared at his experiment shelf, wrote some notes on his pad, sat for a while and a little while longer.

He was still bored.

Henry put his ear against the door of the cupboard to make sure neither Mother nor Georgie was outside. He cracked the door open and double-checked, but he was alone. He closed the door behind him and pulling a hair from his head placed it across the door jamb. If anyone else went in there he would know right away. Quickly he picked himself over for cobwebs so Mother wouldn't ask any awkward questions, and went to look for something else to do.

Georgie was in the garden now, woken from his hibernation and collecting eggs from the chooks. Henry squatted behind the hedge and watched him for a while. He was singing a song to the chickens. 'Little eggs, little eggs, let me have your little eggs, move your funny little legs and let me have your little eggs. Little eggs, little eggs …' Georgie loved the stupid chickens; loved the eggs even more. What he wanted with eggs Henry would never know, but he rolled the things around in his palms, tucked them away in pockets, pulled them out when he thought no one was watching. If it wasn't the eggs and the chickens, it was cats and dogs and frogs and rabbits, ants and bugs.

'Henry!' Georgie had seen him. Henry ducked his head down but it was too late. 'Henry! Eggs!'

'I saw,' Henry said.

'You can have one if you want.'

'You keep them.'

'What are you doing, Henry? Are you doing experiments?'

'Not right now.'

'Some ants were eating a beetle before, do you want to see? They left its wings and everything else went down into their holes. Just hard bits left behind.'

'They ate its guts?'

'All its guts, Henry – you want to see?'

'And its skin, they ate all that?'

'Do beetles have skin, Henry?'

'Wait there,' Henry said. 'Don't follow me! You can't follow me. Wait there. I want to see the ants.'

He slipped quietly through the back door, listening to the sounds of the house. No one was about. He took the hair from its spot across the cupboard door and grabbed his half-rotted, dried-out rat from the highest shelf. It was sticky between his fingers and he wished he'd stolen a rag from the kitchen.

Georgie was singing to the chickens, but he stopped as soon as he saw what Henry had in his hand.

'Who's that, Henry?' Georgie asked, and Henry felt a ripple run through his Mark.

'One of the cats left it. I've been waiting to see its skeleton but it's taking forever. But maybe the ants would eat the other bits and leave the skeleton?'

Henry felt the rushing of ocean water, the swelling of his other self, his own self fading, and his skin tingled with the presence of his Mark as Georgie said, 'Oh, you want to put it on the ants! What a good idea. Let's see what the ants do!'

I am all fingers now, the feel of the animal, small sticky feet, damp sticky fur. We crouch over the dirt pile, the three of us, and their little legs swarm them upwards to the half-rotted beast. Henry grabs towards it, scared to see the whole creature carried away underground, a bubble of heart-cracking regret bursting in his brain, but little brother tells him wait, wait, wait, Henry; watch. Watch.

Tiny teeth they sever the flaps of skin, bite away the strands of hair. Clutched in jaws, passed back and back and back, the animals seethe over and past one another, sniffing and learning, talking and telling and no words, no sound, no ears for these little friends. All smell.

Henry churns with joy. White bones clean and shining in the wet sun. Little brother's 'Who, who, *who* is it, Henry?' tingling still in my heart. We are one bundle of kind-cruel happiness today, aren't we, boy? Little brother fetches a stick, passes it to his Henry, 'Do you want to poke them, Henry?' he asks. Is there any other thing to do but poke a creature on a sunny wet day like today? Of course he does. We do.

Black dots scattering over sand and dragging the last bits of flesh down under with them, the gravel landscape left still and silent. Henry lifts his prize and all of us, we all breathe a sigh of great content. Cradled in his hands, the stick dropped now, its toothy skull still attached to neck bones, spine bones, rib bones, leg bones.

'Thank you, Georgie,' he says and his heart fills with the urge to kiss, which he squashes down deep and instead flashes a smile of generous teeth. 'You should help me put it on its shelf,' he says, and just look at little brother's wriggle of joy. In we trot, into the house, depleted of Mother, Father, wandering sailors and just we three crammed into the cupboard. Georgie on his highest tips of toes to see the top shelf, the sprawled corpses of small souls.

'Did you ever put eggs there?' he asks, and Henry tips a little more towards love. 'What happens to the oldest, oldest of eggs?' says Georgie, and Henry promises he will find out – first, chickens but oh if life is kind, if fate is smiling, sparrows too and crows, currawongs and magpies, the butcherbirds that swoop on tiny wrens and gut their children. All eggs, all in a line, all stinking and exploding and spraying colours never seen before from this end to that.

'Good idea, Georgie,' he says. 'And Georgie,' he says, 'when you bang yourself next time, you know, on your knee or your elbow or your head? When you bang yourself and get a scab, can I have the scab?' He unscrews the lid of the jar and

Georgie, solemnly, looks inside and accepts the responsibility he has been given. 'Always, Henry,' he says.

'Georgie!' Mother calls from the kitchen. 'Henry! Where are you, boys?' They hear the back door open and Mother's call across the garden. She thinks they are hidden behind the chook shed, and both boys smile at the trick they've played. They hold quiet, still in this tiny moment. 'I'll go,' says Georgie. 'Sit here, shh, I'll go and you escape,' and Henry presses little brother's hand in his just for a moment, a second of warm skin. Then Georgie is off and Henry is gone, gone, gone, out of the front door and over the fence.

*

Henry wished just Joe had come with him. Or just Mick. But it'd been both of them there, outside the baker, and when they'd asked him what he was up to he'd said, 'Going down to Semaphore.' 'We'll come too,' they'd said, and they'd dropped the end of the pie they were sharing into the road and Henry had seen a rat creep out and drag it under a box.

He could have said he was on his way home and left them there but sometimes he wondered what it would be like to be one of those boys at school who ran in a gang, who he'd see sometimes on a Saturday afternoon or even a Tuesday evening in a huddle where they shouldn't be, crouched over something or other that his mother usually steered him away from.

So he'd said Semaphore and they'd said they'd come too and he'd imagined, for a minute, what it might be like on Monday to have Joe and Mick come over to him outside school and say, 'Don't go home, come with us. We're going on an adventure.' And he and they and five other boys would light out for who knows where and come back muddy and hungry and Mother would be angry but she'd know he was getting too big now to yell at, not with all those other big boys there with him, standing in the yard, watching as he went inside.

But now they were here at the rock pools. Henry had a line out and he'd got a gull to come ever so close to the end of it but Mick and Joe just wouldn't shut up. They threw things at each other and the birds, they'd chucked a rock in the rock pool to try and crush a crab scuttling there. They didn't know that if you were slow, and quiet, you could wall a crab into a corner and then you could trap it in your hand and it was yours. Do what you want with it. Put it in your pocket and feel it scratch against your leg. Leave it in a teacher's drawer. Ask its secrets. Draw its tiny hands.

Or crush it with a rock. But first you had to catch it. Like the gull. Once it was theirs they could do whatever they wanted with it, so why throw rocks and yell at it now?

The bird flew off and Henry pulled the line back in.

'You have to be quiet,' he told them.

'What?' Joe said.

'You have to be a bit quieter, if you want to catch a gull,' Henry said.

'Who says we want to catch a gull? I want to bloody kill it, just hit it with a rock,' Joe said. 'Chuck rocks at 'em till one of 'em falls out of the sky – why don't we do that?'

'We could fill this pool up with rocks,' said Mick, 'and watch all the fish get squashed.'

'We're meant to be catching a gull!' Henry said.

'Who says?' Joe asked him. 'Who says that's what we're doing?'

'Me,' Henry said. 'I do. We came down here to catch a gull. That's why we came here!'

'Who died and made you boss?' Joe asked.

'Yeah,' said Mick, 'why would we do what you want?'

'Because it's my adventure,' Henry said. 'And you came on it. So you have to be quiet while we catch the gull.' He turned back towards the rock pool and scanned the sand for hungry birds.

'Shhhh!' Joe hissed into his ear, 'Shhhh!' Then he spun around and around yelling, 'Everyone be quiet! We're in the nursery and baby Henry needs to sleep.'

'Don't cry, baby Henry,' Mick said, and threw a rock that bounced and stopped just by Henry's toe.

'Be quiet, Mick! Baby Henry needs to sleep!' and Joe started making crying noises, wah, wah, wah, and Mick was laughing so hard that a little bit of pie came back up into his mouth and he spat it in the rock pool where a tiny fish snatched it away into a crack.

Henry rolled the fishing line up, put it in his pocket and walked away. Joe and Mick kept laughing at his back until he couldn't hear them anymore. When he turned around he could see they were trying to push each other into the water and Mick was knee-deep and stumbling and would probably tumble in any second now.

He walked to the end of the jetty where he lay flat on his stomach, chin on his hands and the boards pressing deep into his fingers. He hung his head over the end and looked upside down into the water. There were no sharks. Silver fish flickered by. He closed one eye, tried to see inside their minds. He dropped his line into the water, baited with a piece of bread and jam. The bread went soft and floated to the surface where a gull swooped down and away with it.

'You can use some of my bait if you want,' a woman said behind him, above him.

Henry rolled over onto his back and let the sky blind him for a moment, propped himself up onto his elbows. The woman was a black shadow against the white sky. He blinked, blinked again.

'You've got fish guts on your lapel,' she said. 'You could use those instead of bread.'

He blinked. It was Mrs Gallwey, from next door, sat on

a vegetable crate and dangling a line into the sea. He pulled himself up to his knees to look in the tin bucket at her side.

'Big fish,' he said.

'Gar,' she said. 'Good spot for them. You'd know that, though.'

'I mostly get flatties,' he told her. 'Me and Father. Once we got a shark, though, a little one. We cut it up and Mother stewed it with turnips and onions and greens and I got to have one piece by itself, fried, so I could just eat it and think about how I ate a shark.'

'Good shark fishing in Sydney,' she told him. 'You should try it some time. They catch man-eaters there.'

'You could eat a shark that ate a man?' Henry sat down by the bucket and dangled his feet over the water. 'Really?'

'I heard once,' she said, pulling her line in and rebaiting her hook, 'about a shark they pulled in off Newport beach. A big one, almost ten foot long, and when they cut it open a little girl fell out with its innards. No one ever claimed her but they said it was probably this English girl, fell off a ship on her way out to Sydney with her family, way off the heads. Guess she finally made it to New South Wales.'

She threw her line back in and nudged a soggy roll of newspaper towards him with her foot. 'There's bait in there,' she said. 'Pop a bit on your hook, why don't you.'

Imagine being that little girl. Tumbling through the water, over and over and over and the water around you churned by the giant ship as it sailed away, away, away from you. Then quiet. Still. So quiet. You pop to the surface and there is nothing, nothing, nothing. Water. An ocean of quiet. So cold. Your coat heavy around you, it pulls you down. Before the air is squeezed from your lungs there it is, huge and grey, the bleak joy of its broadened teeth. You turn into nothing but in the second before you are full of the whole world.

'Boy. Henry, is it?'

Henry nodded. 'Yes, ma'am.'

'Pop some bait on your hook.'

He did, and sat there, line and legs dangling.

'Missus Gallwey,' he said, 'have you seen any other boys in attics?'

'Others?'

'Not just your baby,' he said. 'Other ones. Grown boys, like me.'

'Do you think Ivan lives in the attic?' she asked, and he remembered the baby's name: Ivan.

'He lives in a box in the attic.'

'Does he now,' she said.

'Yes,' Henry said. 'Are there others, do you know? Or in cellars?'

'In Port Adelaide, do you mean?' she asked him.

'Yes. I was thinking it would be good to make a gang, like a pirate gang perhaps. To roam the streets and perhaps set sail. We could steal a boat.'

'But you need boys,' she said, and Henry nodded. 'You don't know any boys who would make good pirates?'

'None.'

A pirate would need to be brave and quiet and most importantly to do as he was told, when Henry told him.

'I see. So boys hidden in cellars or attics would be the ticket. For your gang. Boys with no history or family or schooling.'

'That's right,' Henry said.

'If I see any others,' she told him, 'I'll let you know.'

'Thank you,' Henry said.

'Do you want Ivan?' she asked. 'I'm trying to find him a good home. Perhaps a pirate ship.'

'Too small,' Henry said, and Mrs Gallwey agreed because of course he was. Ivan was just a child.

'Oh, I have a fish!' Henry said, and he pulled in his line and he did have a fish, a whiting, yellow on the tips of its fins as it wriggled and thrashed and fought.

'Will you do it yourself?' Mrs Gallwey asked him. Henry said he would, and she passed him the knife and he drove it through the fish's skull. It was still. Henry put it in the tin bucket and rebaited his hook.

'That's a lovely fish,' she said. 'Your mother will be very pleased with that.'

A while later the sun went down. Mrs Gallwey walked home with him, Henry carrying the bucket, though when they were almost at his gate he said that if she wanted she could keep the whiting, perhaps for Ivan. She shook his hand and said she would.

Mother kissed his face and told him tea was ready, could he please wash his hands. She rubbed at the fish guts on his jacket, smacked him gently on his behind.

6

George heard from Mrs Ann Avage.

'Dear sir,' the letter said, and continued in that cold way. 'I assume you have found my address from *The Register*. I do not welcome your correspondence. Shipmates we may have been, but that time is gone now: a decade passed or more. I will not think on it. I know nothing of the physical symptoms you describe, beyond what a physician could already have diagnosed. Please do not write to me again. I appreciate your condescension in this matter,

Mrs Ann Avage.'

George tore it in half then in half again. It was not her. Black-hearted and avaricious she may be; an otherworldly witch, even. But she was not this kind of cut-crystal bitch. For good measure he tore the pieces even smaller, then dropped them in the fireplace.

He heard also from the woman calling herself Miss Bridget

Ledwith of Morphett Vale. She simpered and cajoled, asked that he meet her in Adelaide, could she pay his fare? Perhaps dinner? He disposed of that letter similarly.

But then a reply came to his advertisement.

'George,' it said, and he felt momentarily hollowed out by the familiarity. He pulled the rough draft of the advertisement from where he had hidden it. No, he had not mentioned his name. Mr Hills on the return address, of course, but not George.

'George, your mystery is solved. I am she. Rest your weary head. Let me know when and where we can meet and I will remove the spell. I only did it to bind you to me. I had always hoped you would one day seek me out. Your one and only Bridget.'

He should tear this too, and burn it. He crumpled it into a ball and threw it in the cold ashes. Retrieved and smoothed it flat, smearing the desktop grey. He turned it upside down and right way up and it made no more or less sense seen either way.

Bridget. George. The spell. She knew. It must be her, surely. Who other could know? No one other. What would it cost him to meet her? Nothing. A fare into Adelaide perhaps. He checked the envelope for a return address and saw it was care of the postmaster in Unley. Perhaps a little more, then. Or perhaps everything: wife, children, home, job, mind, legs to walk on and arms to lift. Eyes to see, teeth to chew. She could lure him to her so he could never return but must live on always as her slave. She could destroy him utterly and toss him back into the ocean. Or she could return the scraps of his health and sanity and let him rejoin the living. She could tell him that the worst of what he had done out there was a dream, perhaps, or if not a dream, only what anyone else would have done. That he was human still. Not monster: human.

'Will you meet me,' he wrote, his hand not particularly steady, and he tried to think of somewhere that no one he knew would see him. William was his only true fear. William who thought nothing of a ride in to Adelaide to visit the Institute Museum, the library. He could not risk North Terrace, despite its convenience for the railway station. He thought of William pulling that newspaper story from his pocket all those years back and still felt a little sick. The man was too clever by half. 'Will you meet me,' he started again with a fresh piece of paper, having smudged the previous one, 'at Victoria House in the Botanic Gardens, by the waterlily, at two o'clock on Thursday the 9th of August.' Two weeks – that would give her time to reply, to change her mind, for him to cover his tracks. Would they need a way to recognise one another? Surely not, he thought. He would know her anywhere, even from a glance at an upstairs window, drunk.

Her reply arrived four days later. 'George,' she said, 'I walked by you today on the street. Didn't you know me?

My arm brushed yours and I am sure you caught my eye for a moment. I have been near you, watching you, since first I saw your notice in the newspaper. We do not need a physical place and time to meet. I am always with you. Close your eyes, go inside yourself, and you will find me there on a deeper plane. Call my name and I will come. Always. Always. Bridget.'

He checked the return address. She was definitely still in Unley. What was she on about? He double-checked no one else had crept into the room, then closed his eyes and tried to go inside himself, but within three seconds he felt an utter fool and opened them again.

'Miss Ledwith,' he wrote, and this time his hand was firmer, 'please stay away from my house. It would not do for me to be seen with you. It would do you no favours either.' Didn't she value her privacy? He had thought she did. 'I understand you are a mystical creature but please condescend to lower yourself to the material. I am a simple steward and not familiar with the goings-on of higher beings. Can you meet me in the Victoria House? If the 9th of August is now too soon, please let me know a better day. Yours, George Hills.'

'Henry!' he called. 'Henry, are you home?'

The boy didn't answer.

He checked the kitchen and the boys' bedroom and the backyard but there was no sign of him. When he went back into the house, he saw Henry shutting the cupboard door behind him.

'Were you in the cupboard?' he asked.

'In the? Oh, in the cupboard! No. No.' Henry looked at his feet, then looked up and smiled confidently. 'Were you looking for me, Father?'

'I know you were in the cupboard. We can discuss that later. Come into my office.'

George could hear Henry dragging his feet, and he told him to pick them up and walk properly.

'Shut the door behind you,' George said. 'I need to talk with you about that mark you have.'

'Mark?' The boy was playing innocent.

'On your back.'

Henry nodded.

'You still have it?'

Henry nodded.

'Does it hurt ever? Itch?'

'No. It's fine, it's no problem.'

George could see Henry's fingers move to touch his mark, then drop back to his side.

'Take your shirt off for me,' George said. 'Come on then, I'm not going to hurt you.'

He turned the boy around, gently, his arms still so thin and brittle, and ran his fingertips over the sprawling birthmark. Somewhere inside him – and it was not his brain but somewhere lodged inside his guts – that rough coolness felt under his fingers the way that she had, clutched against him and the only talisman he had left against madness, death, despair.

'That hurts,' Henry said, and George released his grip on the boy's bony shoulder, leaving purple fingerprints on the skin. He took Henry's shirt from his lap and handed it back to him, gestured for him to pull it back on. Henry's face was dark and George couldn't tell whether from shame or anger or something else.

'Your shoulder is all right?' George muttered.

Henry nodded.

'Well, good.'

George shuffled some things around on his desk, then realised his letter to Bridget had been uncovered and rapidly reshuffled everything.

'Do you have bad dreams?' he asked his son. 'Strange dreams? Ever?'

'Strange …? Sometimes things are chasing me and I can't run, or I'm at school and I have to go up in front of the class and I don't have any clothes on.'

George flushed with relief at the normality of it, smiled at the boy. 'I still have that dream and I hardly went to school at all. Haven't been there for at least twenty-five years.'

His smile faded as he remembered he was not to let himself be comforted. He tried to explain himself. 'Maybe, I mean, do you have dreams, times, where you don't feel like you? Where it's as though someone else is in your brain?'

'I don't have those dreams.'

'Not thoughts, feelings, either?'

'No, never.'

'Well, all right then. Still, it has to go.' He gestured towards Henry's shoulder. 'That thing. I'm having it removed.'

'Oh! Please don't!' The boy had half got up from his chair, and his fingers flew again to the collar of his shirt, dove inside.

'What's the problem, boy? You want to keep it?'

Why would he want to keep it? Why would he want to clutch such a thing so close to his skin?

'It's …' George wanted to say that it was a monster, a curse, a demonic possession. He stopped himself. 'It's a deformity.'

'But …' Henry sat back again. 'Won't it hurt?'

'Hurt? No, it won't hurt, if that's what you're so worried about. It won't hurt. It will go. It will just … be gone. Are you crying?'

'No!' Henry dropped his hand from his face and took a deep breath. 'No, Father.'

'Good.'

George sat quietly for a while and Henry rose as though to leave the room. George stopped him. 'The thing is, you can't say anything to your mother. Don't go running to her asking where your mark has gone, all right? Just keep quiet.

She'll notice sooner or later, but just act as though you know nothing. You understand?' He knew that Henry lied all the time, to both of them.

'When will it happen?'

'I still want to know what you're up to in that cupboard – don't think you got away with that. Thursday. Probably Thursday. Never you mind. But you tell me when it goes.'

'Yes, Father.'

'Off you go, then. Try to be a good boy for a while, will you?'

Henry didn't answer, but he left and shut the door behind him, and after a while George could hear him yelling out to his little brother about some kind of experiment.

He folded the letter, slipped it into an envelope, wrote her name and 'Deeper Plane', then crossed it out so it could still be read and readdressed it to the Unley post office. Funny, he thought. Pretty funny. Could he get Henry to post it? Best not, chances are the boy would open it. Well, maybe the walk would do him good. Maybe Eliza could come for a walk with him. He had some business letters to post too, Home business. Slip the letter in with those and she'd never notice. A little walk with his wife would be lovely.

'Eliza!' he yelled, gathering up the envelopes and slipping them into the inner pocket of his jacket. 'Are you here, Eliza?'

Her head popped around the door, her hair all ruffled from one thing or another, and he couldn't help smile. She held baby Wills on her hip and George reached out to stroke the child's cheek.

'Hello, lovely wife,' he said.

'Hello, dearest husband. You yelled?'

'I yelled? That wasn't yelling. A gentle call. A soft song.'

'A terrific yell.'

'Well, perhaps I was overexcited at the prospect of seeing you. Will you come for a walk with me to the post office? Chances are I will need to steal some flowers from this garden and that and perhaps you could help me carry them.'

Eliza smiled back. 'Of course. Just let me comb my hair and put some clothes on this baby,' she said and George heard her call to the boy, 'Henry, can you watch your brother, please?'

7

The curved glass of Victoria House was hurting his eyes, gleaming in the low wintery sun. He sat on a bench at a safe distance, watching people enter and leave the glasshouse. He remembered Eliza had once loved to come here when the waterlily was blooming. She and Sarah would catch the train in and meet two of their old schoolfriends to see the lily, then lunch and some shopping. Why didn't she do that anymore? The children, probably. Three children would be too many to drag around the hot, noisy streets of Adelaide. No sense in their heads, either: they'd probably fall in the lily pond and drown. *Maybe Wills has some sense,* he reflected. *He might turn out all right. Those other boys, though, honestly.* He didn't doubt he was their father – no one could think such a thing of Eliza – but he couldn't see himself in them at all. Henry was more like William, in love with words and ideas. Someone should steer him towards a sensible idea or two;

the ones he had now were largely crazy. And Georgie, his namesake. That boy was off with the fairies. The number of times George had seen him involved in a serious conversation with a butterfly ...

Women passing, each of them much like the last, their long skirts and high collars, their long hair bound high on their heads. A hat here and there. Cinched in at the waist, raised up at the heel. How would he know the woman? He'd know her because his face would feel like it was on fire and his guts would churn green bile. That's how he'd know.

'George, this isn't the lily pond,' she said as she sat down next to him, and his face kept its normal composition and so did his guts.

He forced himself not to turn and stare. He forced himself not to bawl fury at whoever this woman was.

Instead, 'Is that you, Miss Ledwith?' he asked.

'I believe you suggested we meet by the lily pond at two o'clock. It's after two o'clock and you're still sitting out here watching the door.'

'I wanted to surprise you.'

'Wait while I close my eyes then.'

He did turn to look and she had closed her eyes.

'Boo,' he said.

He knew this woman but not the way he knew that woman.

'You look different,' he said.

She opened her eyes. 'I'm wearing clothes. If you want to, we can change that.'

'Not right now.' He might keep that as a possibility. 'It was too warm in there,' he said, meaning the glasshouse. 'I had to get some fresh air. You found me anyway, so it doesn't matter.'

'No, it doesn't matter. You look well, George.'

'I'm not dying of exposure, which may be why.'

'Old, though. You definitely look old.'

'Thank you. Everyone's been looking for you, did you know? Or at least they were. For years. Newspapers, lawyers, wellwishers. Why have you come out of hiding for me? I don't have any money, if that's what you're after.'

'I knew. None of them interested me. You, on the other hand –' she touched him lightly on the arm – 'have always interested me. We were quite the team back then, weren't we? Quite ...' she paused, perhaps looking for the right word, 'tight.'

'I suppose. Of course, it would probably have been better had I died. Rather than team up with you, that is.'

'George! So bleak. Here we are on this beautiful day, the glorious young city of Adelaide buzzing around us, all the ladies out walking, a pretty girl by your side. How could you wish yourself dead?' The smile went out of her voice and she turned to look him in the eye. 'Not everyone would survive a thing like that, George. The facts bear me out – most did not. But we did. Because we are made of special stuff. Strong stuff. We do what's needed. There should be more like you and me.'

'You're quite convincing, but I can still tell that you're not her. Who are you?'

'Would you like to interrogate me, make me prove I am who I say I am? I am, George. Do you want me to tell you about the scar you have running from your knee up your thigh?' and she actually ran a fingertip along his very scar.

'Yes, very impressive. I don't wish to interrogate you. You say you're Bridget Ledwith. There must be ten other women across the colonies say the same. The reason I'm meeting you here —'

'Rather than by the lily pond, where you said you would meet me.'

'The reason I'm meeting you here, rather than meeting any of those other Bridgets, is that you seem to know you're an evil spirit from the bowels of hell. The others think Bridget Ledwith is a woman.'

'Spirit woman, you said, George. You did not specify evil. And nor am I. I may be able to dwell on a deeper plane and to affect the inner workings of your mind and heart, but let us not leap to any conclusions that I am evil.' She leaned in closer, almost whispering in his ear. 'Do you want to talk about how I can help you sleep at night?'

'Do you have any party tricks other than the scar?' he

said, and removed her hand from his thigh. 'Stand up in front of me, will you?'

'I'm not a shop mannequin, George.'

'Will you just do it?'

She stood.

'Turn, slowly.'

At the nape of her neck her deep brown hair, the colour of Bridget's, was betrayed by blond curls escaping from beneath a wig. Why would he be surprised? He had known all along it wasn't her.

'Well then, sit down. Your hair hasn't changed, anyway. Your face is close enough, though you've enough powder on there to choke a miner. As to the shape of you, who would know? You're all corseted up and covered in lawn and muslin or whatever that nonsense is, so let's leave that be. So what's your plan for lifting the curse of the *Admella*?'

'Finally,' she said, and she sat next to him again. 'Can you tell me a little more about what afflicts you?'

'You placed the curse,' he said. 'Surely you remember what afflictions you chose.'

'You cannot sleep at night, you have trouble breathing. I did not place the curse, George. We all have it. The curse was carried in the boat. I saved you from the worst of it. I took your heart and your mind in my loving spiritual hands and guided you through those long days and nights. You wish to be where those other drowned souls are now? Oh, I'm sure you imagine them sleeping soft in the bosom of heaven, having cast off the cares of the earth. It's a fantasy, George. They're thrashing about in agony far worse than anything you can imagine.'

'But they —'

'But they didn't eat some other human's flesh – I know. Part of the curse, George, that we did that. It wasn't our fault, the ship made us do it. That ship was possessed. It ate the souls of the wrecked. I saved you, I kept you alive, I got you back to land and let you repair yourself with good works. You have a family now, don't you? Two boys and a girl?'

'Something like that.'

'A wife, a job, an income. You can spend every single day in church if you want to, George – you have time to gain God's forgiveness. None of the dead have that. You have time, time that I bought for you.'

'So I should just go to church and all this will be fixed?' Church was for Christmas, Easter and whenever Eliza got a bee in her bonnet and made him go. If they were going to talk church it was time he went home.

'You can try. I don't believe it will work.'

'Then what?'

'I know an incredible hypnotist. He will —'

'You too?'

'Don't interrupt. While my spiritual gifts are already strong, there were parts of myself even I could not scrub clean. He has helped me do that. That ship, that reef, no longer have any hold over me. We will visit him and he will make you whole.'

'For a considerable sum, I suppose?'

'His rates are perfectly reasonable, particularly when you consider the miracles he can work.'

'Would you mind if we took a turn about the park, Miss Ledwith? My aged joints are stiffening on this bench.'

He felt a little more comfortable walking with the woman than he did sitting like ducks waiting to be found and shot. Walking was explicable. The wife of a friend. They had simply crossed paths and were now strolling and chatting for a spell, catching up on old times.

'Don't these trees cast a beautiful pattern of shadow?' she asked.

'I suppose they do. So this hypnotist – boyfriend of yours, is he?'

'I beg your pardon?'

'Is he your man? You take me in there, like some rube hick, he waggles a watch or whatever it is they do these days, I take a little nap, he fleeces me and you split the proceeds? Something like that?'

'Mister Hills! How dare you! I'm a respectable woman.'

'That you certainly are not and nor have you ever been, even if you are who you claim to be. Either you're some kind of ocean-going witch-siren, or you're a shyster. Your choice, Miss Ledwith.'

'I think you're a little hysterical. Now look, George. You have problems, and I am trying to help. Of course there may be some expense involved, but for me that is neither here nor there. I simply replied to your call for assistance and am doing my utmost to help you get well. What is there in it for me? Nothing but knowing a fellow shipmate is in good hands. We did have something once, George. I am driven by –' she paused – 'let's call it affection.'

'Yes, very nice. I do need to get home soon, so perhaps we could come clean with one another. I know you're not Bridget Ledwith. That is disappointing for me. However it is that you've come across the information, you clearly know that I carry a weight of sin from my time on that wreck, and I had honestly hoped you may be able to help me lift that weight. Unfortunately, you have turned out to be some kind of confidence artist and not the very strange woman I spent eight days with on that infernal reef.'

'Who else would know about your scar? Who else would know the things you did to stay alive? If you want to throw away your last chance at salvation, then that is your choice. But you need not accuse me of lying!' The woman was raising her voice quite effectively and drawing some very curious stares. She'd stopped dead in the path, her arms crossed over her breasts and a ferocious stare on her face. Whoever she was, she wasn't afraid of a little publicity.

'Oh!' George said. 'I know how it is I know you!'

'From the *Admella*! Are you losing your mind?'

'No! I saw you last year. A musical production, with my brother-in-law. You had the lead. A fabulous performance, we both said so. That girl is quite something, I remember thinking it. And you still are. What a privilege to meet you in the flesh.' George grinned widely and held out his hand.

'Oh, I told Davey this would never work,' she muttered. 'I couldn't convince you Miss Ledwith had taken to the stage, I suppose?'

'I shouldn't think so.'

'Well, that's that then. Are you very rich?'

'Me? No. You thought I was rich? You really did mean to fleece me. You're a terrible person, Miss … Miss …'

'Jarvis. Alice.'

'You are a terrible person, Miss Alice Jarvis. Do you spend much of your spare time preying on desperate men?'

'Very little. You are the first.' She slumped onto a nearby bench. 'Are you going to call the police?'

'Come off it.' He sat beside her. 'How did you know about the scar?'

'Davey remembered. David Peters. He was on the wreck with you. He's my man. He saw your notice in the paper. You shouldn't have put your name on it, George.'

'I didn't!'

'You put your name in your mailing address. The rest was very easy to figure out. There was only one woman survived that wreck, George. Anyone reading the notice would have known who you meant. I'm surprised you haven't heard from the real Miss Ledwith, ordering you to stop smearing her good name. Or have you?'

'You're the third I've heard from, but the other two weren't even convincing enough to get me out of the house. I don't think she actually exists.'

'No one knows what became of her, do they?'

'She's a monster. That's why. She isn't human.'

'This is a very strange obsession you have, Mister Hills.'

'You'd have it too if you'd seen what I'd seen. I think I remember Peters. I suppose that's how you know about ...' and he mimed putting a piece of meat to his mouth.

She nodded.

'Hm.' Yes, he had a vague picture of Peters in his head. 'He was the fireman?' he asked.

'That's him. Though not anymore. Like you, Mister Hills, he has struggled. More than you. You have a job and a family. He can't manage either.'

'So he thought he'd try to get some of mine.' But George was sympathetic. It was a filthy feeling, having seen what they'd seen. 'He was the hypnotist?'

She nodded.

'So, what? I'd keep coming back for more and more sessions, looking for a cure, and I'd keep paying, and you two would spend the money until I finally admitted I couldn't be fixed?'

'Something like that. Or perhaps you'd fall for my charms and we would find a way to blackmail you.'

'Savage, Miss Jarvis. Unpleasant of the both of you.'

'Well –' she smiled – 'had you chosen the latter it would not have been entirely unpleasant for you.'

'I can imagine,' he said, 'and later, I probably will, at least once or twice.'

'You needn't imagine.' She held his gaze. 'Perhaps I could make all this up to you. My rooms aren't far from here —'

'I thought you lived in Unley?'

'Unley! I certainly couldn't afford that. No, that was just a respectable mailing address. I'm around the corner, near the theatre. Would you like to pop back? I wouldn't mind seeing that scar in real life.'

George stilled the insistent voice in his trousers suggesting that there was no real reason not to, why not after all, she seemed like a fine young woman, no one would ever know, she owed him that, and so on. 'You shouldn't have warned me about the blackmail. Now I know that, I'm a little reluctant. No, thank you, I'll head home now. But look, give this to Peters.' He pulled a small wad of notes from his pocket. 'I know how rough it can be. Don't spend it on yourself, mind. Give it to your man.'

She dropped the cash in her purse. 'Come and see me on the stage again some time, Mister Hills. Bring your brother. Is he as handsome as you?'

'Brother-in-law. He's a wiry sort. Impressive moustache, though. Do you like an impressive moustache? Perhaps you could take him off my hands. I'm sure he'd be up for a bit of hypnotism. Yes, might just do that, young lady. We might just do that.'

'And let me know if you find this ocean-going witch-siren. I'm fascinated.'

'It's not funny,' he said. 'She's destroying my family.' And as he watched Alice Jarvis swan her way out of the park, heads turning to watch her, he felt the weight of it all descend on him again. Perhaps he should have gone to see her fake hypnotist. Perhaps it would have helped. Without a doubt, he should have followed her home. For the last half-hour he'd felt almost normal; another half-hour wrapped around her skin and he might have remembered how it was to be a human man. Instead he stepped back into all that was waiting for him. His life, still unchanged.

8

Henry lay face down on his bed, his fingers brushing across his Mark, waiting for the moment it would vanish. He slid a fingernail under the edge of it, felt it peel away and wrap itself tight around his finger. His oldest friend. The twist in his brain; the always-suck of it. His mother's eyes glancing off him and away. His father, revolted. How would it be, to have skin that felt dry inside and out? To have feet that felt only dirt?

He'd been fighting the oceanic tug of it for many months now, trying to force his brain to stay here on dry land, where his body lived. But today might be the last time. He let himself go and found he was not in the oceanic depths but instead flung out, out, out into the black. And there, just a speck of it, was a planet, formed in the perfect spot in a vast, cold universe.

Spinning through the black he watched it shift and

change - rock planet, ice planet, ocean planet, land planet and then in a haze of clouds and under the eye of one warm star it became ocean, land and sky. Just right.

There were creatures – tiny, so many – a swarm of them struggling and fighting and out of them came babies and blood and all the heat of that one warm star turned to grass and to muscle and to life.

Teeth tearing throats. The guts of a rabbit are the eyes of a newborn dingo pup are the food that fuels the towering termite nest are the shade where a small skink rests. In a river, in a pond, in the shifting desert sand, in mountain rock and the cold ice of glaciers and in one yard of earth.

The disease that devoured one and passed over another. The rat's little body all thick with ants. The apple cores food for worms. All of it, life.

The great joyous throb of it.

He plunged into the swarming ocean, felt its wriggling abundance. Slumped and lay soft on the currents of it, drifting. Henry sounded the ancient depths of his Mark – like this today and yesterday and tomorrow and always. No shadows fell, no teeth snapped and there was a stillness amid the frenzy. Henry felt his place in it – just to be this boy and never wonder why or who or how to be better, braver, otherwise. Just to be and to love. To notice it fresh every day. Not to fear it leaving; to know it always was and always will be, and that when this body stops and rots and makes itself food that still it will all go on just like this, just like always. Tiny tragedies, tiny triumphs and none of it meaning a thing against the great still monstrousness of forever and always. This always ocean, this always world, these always stars, this stretching, boundless, eternal universe. This quiet space.

'You can let go of that thing,' his father called as he passed down the hallway, 'it's not going anywhere. You're stuck with it. And your mother says to go and fetch her eight sausages.'

Henry's head broke the surface of the water and he breathed and breathed, lungs not gills, and his eyes stung so from the salt that he didn't see them, there underwater, his father's boots stomping and smashing and crushing as the dirt poured in over everything and broke the universe into past, present, future.

9

At the butcher, Henry rubbed his wet, dirty face on his sleeve and took his place in the queue. 'Let it be Mister Sidney, let it be Mister Sidney, let it be Mister Sidney,' he chanted to himself, no idea what he'd do if he got to the front and Mr Felton was serving.

'What're you after, boy?' Mr Sidney called him out of the line, round to the side of the counter.

'Special order, sir.'

'What's that?'

'Special. Order.'

'For your mam, is it?'

'No, Mister Sidney, for me. I just … oh, never mind,' and Henry felt his eyes begin to leak again with the stupid frustration of it all, these useless grown-ups and their nonsense world.

'Oh!' The apprentice's grin turned wicked. 'Special order.

Wait a moment.' Sidney slipped through the curtain covering the door to the back room, but he was back within seconds. 'Sorry, Hills, nothing left out there today. Mister Felton must have taken it all round to the blood-and-bone man already.'

Henry had been hoping for a head, or maybe even a heart. This was such a terrible day.

'Well, thank you anyway. Just eight sausages then.' He would go walk on the beach maybe. Or run away from home.

'Though if you're not busy after, perhaps you could pop back then.'

'After? After what?'

'Keep your voice down. After … you know. After we close. Can you come back after we close?'

Henry nodded. 'You're getting another beast in? To cut up?'

'Oh, something much better than that. Come back in an hour.' Sidney called to the queue, 'Who's next?'

Henry gave the apprentice the secret sign as he left, but Sidney never could learn the secret sign and just frowned at him.

When Henry got back, at the time the shop was normally closed, Sidney was waiting out the front for him.

'That Felton could do with a lesson in what's right and what's wrong, if you take my meaning. He needs to learn to respect a man, he does. In three more months I'll be eighteen and done with all this and maybe I'll head to Victoria and find my own Welcome Stranger and he can just do his own dirty work.'

Henry didn't really know what Sidney was on about, so he nodded and made his own face look very serious and a little angry.

'It's down here.'

Sidney led him down an alley which ran from Ship Street to an open space beyond. Behind one of the buildings, thick weeds had grown and it looked as though some animals had made nests there.

'In there.' Sidney tipped his chin towards a particularly dense patch of weeds.

'What is it?'

'Go look. You'll soon see.'

Suddenly Henry wished he was at home with Mother, maybe even helping Georgie collect eggs from the hens.

'What's in there?' he asked again.

'Are you feeble? Get in there. Here,' Sidney grabbed a stick from the ground and thrust it at Henry. 'Take this. Poke about a bit.'

It was probably a snake, Henry thought. Snakes were fine. He once had half a snake skeleton in his collection. If Sidney wanted to frighten him with a snake he was going to be sorely disappointed.

'There's nothing there, is there, Mister Sidney?' Henry said, after three or four pokes about in the weeds with the stick and still not a single snake. 'Maybe it's left?'

'Left? It can't leave. Here, give me that.'

Sidney thrashed the stick about in the weeds. 'Ah, here it is! Some dogs must've been at it. Can you see now?'

Henry squatted down, unsure what he was meant to be looking at. It was something dead, no doubt about that: there were maggots seething all over the thing. Sidney knocked at them with the stick, and as they tumbled into the grass Henry saw that they had been feeding on a person's arm. He peered closer.

'Who is it?'

'Who? It's nobody. A swaggie.'

Henry hadn't seen a dead person before. He hadn't expected it would be quite so damp and soft and swollen, or would smell quite as strong. Cats and birds and snakes seemed drier, more like a husk. This was a bit hard to look at. He forced himself to look anyway.

'How'd he get here?'

'Well, I dunno, do I? How would I know?'

'Do you know where his head is?'

'Why so many questions, Hills?' Sidney smacked him across his shin with the stick, and Henry fell back into the dirt. 'Are you done looking?'

Henry was and he wasn't.

'Come on, time to get out of here. Don't go telling no one, all right? Or I'll have to tuck you up with him.' Sidney smiled.

Henry didn't reply and, though he felt like running as fast

as he could, he headed back towards the street at a leisurely stroll, whistling a little.

'He's a good one, isn't he?' Sid yelled after him. 'Beautiful and ripe!' And he laughed like it was the best joke anyone had ever made.

Where would his head have got to? Henry waited until Sid had gone off in the direction of the pub, then went back down into the weeds. How had he got here? Did someone kill him on purpose? Did he just come down here one day, sick, and did he go to sleep and die? You'd still have a head, though, wouldn't you, if that happened. Your head wouldn't rot clean away before the rest of you.

Maybe he'd never had a head.

Maybe the man had stalked around the streets of Port Adelaide at night, just a bloody neck stump on his shoulders. He wouldn't have to eat or drink. He couldn't, could he: no mouth to eat with. Unless maybe he'd caught rats and cats and torn them to bits then pushed the meaty chunks down into his neck hole. Or maybe he'd wring them out till the blood dripped down his open wound!

But what would kill someone like that? What would kill a monster who walked the streets all night without a head? He'd drag a metal pole behind him, clack, clack, clack over the cobblestones, and anyone who heard him would know that was it, they were doomed. There wasn't anyone in Port who could fight a monster like that, a blood-drinking headless monster with a ferocious metal pole. Unless it was another monster. A bigger monster. A fiercer monster. A monster like that would come back to check the headless monster was still dead. And maybe kill it again if it hadn't died properly the first time. Which maybe it hadn't. As soon as dark came he'd be up again, walking the streets and dragging his metal pole behind him, looking for cats to wring for their blood. Or children.

It was after five and the sun was starting to go down and Henry thought it would probably be a good idea to go home. Mrs Gallwey was leaving the pub with a jug of beer, so Henry fell in step beside her. Mick and Joe hissed 'Witch, witch!' from their usual haunt in the doorway of the bakery as they passed, but Mrs Gallwey didn't even look their way.

Henry could hear the fading wails of Mick's best baby impression as they turned the corner. Mrs Gallwey kicked a rock along before her. She didn't seem inclined to speak, but Henry was bursting with the thing he'd just seen.

He tried to think of a way he could talk about it without getting himself in trouble with Sidney.

'Do you know Sidney?' he asked.

'I used to live there,' she said. 'I know it very well.' The rock fell into a drain and she swore quietly.

'The butcher's apprentice?'

'Who?'

The wind off the water was cold, the waves slapping hard

against the piers of the jetty. No one else much was out and all the shops had already closed. It was quiet enough that Henry could hear a horse and carriage coming towards them long before he saw it. It passed them by in a mess of steam and sweat.

'There's a dead swaggie down behind Ship Street,' he said. Mrs Gallwey nodded.

'He doesn't have a head,' Henry said.

'You saw him?' she asked. 'They were talking about him in the pub. Filthy business. Treating him like a freak show.'

'Who is he?' Henry asked.

'Who cares? Nobody cares, Henry, and you won't get far if you do. Dead swaggies, dead blackfellas: the forest that's cleared to till the field of civilisation, young man. Stack them up and get on with the job.'

'But what about all the ghosts?'

'Sorry?'

'All the ghosts. All the headless monsters walking the streets after dark, wringing out the bodies of cats and rats to drink their blood. They won't leave us be.'

'You've seen these ghosts?' Mrs Gallwey stopped at the corner of their street and took a swig from the beer jug.

Henry nodded. 'He carries a metal pole and he drags it behind him when he walks the streets at night. We killed him and he'll never let us be.'

'Is that right?'

'We did it.'

Henry could feel a mountain of corpses shifting inside him, the wet bodies of a billion slaughtered creatures and the headless swaggie tossed on top. He squeezed his eyes shut but it just made the smell of them, the clutching seaweed smell of them, rise up in his nostrils. He shook his head, bent over to breathe, or to vomit – he didn't know which.

'Stop it!' he hissed at his Mark, and then he remembered she was leaving him and he sat down suddenly in the gutter and clutched at his shoulder.

Mrs Gallwey sat beside him and he watched as the bottom of her skirt darkened from the mud.

'You know your mother will probably see you sitting here if you stay much longer,' she said. Henry saw they were out the front of his house. 'And now that I'm sitting here too I can only imagine what people will say. That strange Henry Hills, they'll say. Just like him to be drinking in the gutter with that gypsy witch Beatrice Gallwey. Maybe another few months and it'll be us down the back of Ship Street.' She smiled.

'Missus Gallwey?' He didn't think she was listening. 'Can I ask you a question?'

'I have no doubt,' she said.

'Did you ever see anyone whose skin was theirs and wasn't theirs?'

'Like wearing a mask made from another human's face, do you mean? Or gloves?'

'I …' He couldn't think of a way to explain it, that it was his body and not his body. That it had a mouth but no one else knew. That he could feel under the edges of it but Mother, who touched him every day, thought it was all one with his skin. 'Can I show you?'

Why was he asking her? Because she was strange, and old, and because she'd come from New South Wales and she knew gypsies and because she understood about catching fish and because he had never seen another adult who wasn't drunk sitting in a gutter.

'That depends how far we have to travel. This beer won't drink it itself, and if it does Missus Frome will have my hide.'

'It's here,' he said. 'It's me.'

'In that case, why don't you get yourself out of this gutter and we'll pop over to my place for a bit.'

Henry sat quietly in the kitchen while the beer was poured. Mrs Frome and the man took their beer outside. Henry took off his shirt. Mrs Gallwey held a candle close to see better, and Henry felt the edges of his Mark ripple away from the heat.

'Can you see that?' he asked her.

'It's alive, isn't it,' she said.

He nodded.

'How astonishing,' she said.

'I imagine having another creature living on you creates problems. What does your mother say?' Gallwey asked once his shirt was back on and she'd put a small glass of beer in front of him.

'She says it's nothing to worry about, I'm a healthy, normal boy. She won't look at it. I mean, she sees it but she doesn't see it. She just sees my skin.'

'Do you want it off you?'

'No! No. Sometimes. But no.' He didn't know how much to tell her. 'Father is trying to make it go. He hates it.'

'He knows it's alive?'

'I don't know. But he asks me questions about it. "Does it make you dream evil dreams?" He says he knows someone who will make it vanish. Next week, he's seeing him next week and this person will make it vanish.' Henry gulped the beer, forgetting that was what was in front of him, and gagged and coughed on the bitter taste.

'Does it make you dream evil dreams?'

'No! It's my friend.'

'But you can hear it inside your head, can't you?'

He shouldn't tell her. She was strange but she was a grown-up and grown-ups wanted everything normal and usual and clean. 'I should go. Thank you for the beer.'

'Sit down, sit down. You can go in a minute. First, listen. In Sydney I met a man. American, from Monterey, California. Loved the ocean. You want another glass of beer?'

Henry shook his head.

'He had a mark, like yours, across his back. I thought it was a tattoo. You know what a tattoo is?'

Henry had seen pictures of the fierce Maori warriors of New Zealand and had long thought that once he turned thirteen he would demand a tattoo on his upper lip. He nodded.

'But when I ran my finger across it, it rippled. It lived. It was just that tiny bit cooler than the rest of his skin.' Henry felt his Mark ripple too, its clutch on his skin tighten. 'Aquatic, it was, like yours. Nothing you could pin down, not shaped like a fish or anything, but you knew as soon as you looked hard enough that this had something to do with the ocean. Yours too, isn't it?'

Henry nodded again and felt his Mark seethe and stretch, the edges of it crawling across his back, up his neck, and he wondered if today would be the day it would eat him entirely and all his problems would be gone.

'He said he'd learned long ago to keep his mouth shut about his shade. That's what he called it, his shade. He wanted me to believe it was a tattoo but it wasn't. "Tell me about your shade, Aden," I kept asking. I think that was his name. Aden. Hm, maybe it was Adrian. No, no – I'm pretty sure it was Aden. You'd probably like me to get on with the story, wouldn't you?' she said. 'Yes, well, first I'm going to need more beer. Why don't you run outside and get Missus Frome to fill this up for me?' She handed him her glass.

He stood up from the table and it was like tearing skin from flesh, the effort of it. His Mark did not want to be carried up, away; she wanted here and more. But he dragged the two of them from the chair and out the door.

Outside, the old lady and that man he didn't know were lighting a fire on the ground, even though the night was warm. He didn't want to interrupt, so he filled the glass himself and went back in.

'Don't suppose you saw Ivan while you were out there, did you? I'm not sure he's had any dinner.'

Henry shook his head.

'Never mind, another ten minutes won't do him any harm. I'm sure he'll let me know if he's hungry.' She had a drink. 'This shade – Aden said he'd had it as long as he remembered, and he would've been in his late forties when I knew him.'

'How did they come together?' Henry asked.

'When he was small he used to swim in a big rock pool near his home in Monterey. One day he'd felt a shiver across his skin, he said. A kind of swooning feeling. Not as though anything had touched him, but like his skin was changing into something else. And when he ran his fingers over his back it felt different. Not very different, not so different anyone else would notice, but different in the way you would notice if you'd got a little cut on your lip or a flake of skin sticking out on your nose.'

Henry touched the aching stretch across his back and didn't know how it might be without it.

'The strange thing, he told me, was that he started knowing all these things he'd never known before. Not facts. Not things like how much President Lincoln weighed or the cost of tea in China. Feelings, mostly. How it felt to live underwater. Other lives, he said. Other ways of thinking.'

'We live together in the underwater world,' Henry said. 'A planet all ocean: always was, always will be.' Henry's Mark was throbbing, rippling, pulsing. 'Another brain in my brain, another me in me, maybe she is me and I am ... I don't know.' It almost hurt to talk; he could feel that brain in his now, squeezing out his thoughts.

Mrs Gallwey talked more, like nothing was going wrong. 'Did you pick yours up in the ocean?' she asked.

He shook his head. 'Always there,' he said. 'Since I was born.' He had to go, he had to be somewhere quiet and dark, let his brain fill with whatever it needed to fill with. 'I have to go.'

'Well, wait up a minute,' Mrs Gallwey was saying, 'are you sure you're well enough to ...'

Sharp in his head as he ran for the door, one question: 'Is he still in Sydney?'

'Is he ... ? Oh, Aden! No. This was a long time ago, before I was married. His ship went back to California. He was ...'

But Henry was over the fence and behind the hedge and into the dark and the rush, the rush of his mind.

There is another, there is another, there is another, there is another.

I am not alone.

CURED

1

There is another.

There is another half a planet away and I live on a little boy who has never been further than the edge of the ocean. How to propel him foot by small foot over half a planet of city, road, ocean, deep river and mountain and desert and lake? I take him to the ocean edge and we watch the boats and I tell him to just put one foot down then another, walk your way onto that ship and we will be on there and gone but he will not.

We rattle about in our house, school, street, we laugh and run and curl for sleep, but I will not let him be. One night he takes a stick and beats me with it to silence me and gives himself so much pain his sheet is bloody and his mother frets.

Take me to the ocean edge, I tell him. Take yourself, he tells me, but his face is grimy-smeared from tears.

I could take myself – I could swim, stumble, fly. I could. But I have been almost a whole lifetime with him, my Henry, my boy. On my own planet I grew to adulthood. Here I have slid down into old age. One whole life, there in my waterworld: a life of every day the same. Then one whole other life, feeling this boy grow under me, learning language tucked here beneath his ear, learning where to put words, thoughts, hands, feet. One safe place smashed by their dirty boots. A new one found – flimsy, see-through, dry and desolate, but still. Still.

Take yourself, he tells me again, and this time his eyes stay dry.

I cling a little harder, bury myself safe inside his shirt, his mind. But I know I did not come all this way to hide among the clothes of humans.

I unwrap myself from him and remember myself back into fleet-footed fur. I am stiff and creaky from long years of stillness. He laughs as he watches and I see his face is not altogether dry. A tentacle unwinds from my grey-furred back and he strokes it back into a vanishing place. He picks me up and holds us nose against nose, my small heart bumping against his thumbs, my life in his hands. He laughs again. 'Kitty.' My claws cling sharp in his shirt and a part of me tears away as cat-shaped I wriggle in his hands until my feet are back on ground. When he calls after me I close my ears and run for the ships.

My scampering feet and swift teeth are welcome here. My hardened feline heart. I slaughter rats in the barrels, in the beds. I perch lofty and wind-blown and I clean rough between my claws. I wait and wait and wait and then – finally – we creak and shift, thrown out into the open water.

We are one day and not even one night ocean-going when a rolling tussle with a big fellow, stripy haunches and torn in the ear, tosses me over the edge and into the waves. I am flashing fish, star, worm as I tumble down until I feel my old self creep across my skin and there I am, tentacled and soft and I breathe in over my gills and jet out and I am flying. Then I am not.

It is deep ocean here where I have fallen. I am out of strength out of practice. I sink and sink and the centre of this earth pulls me closer, closer. The dark closes tighter and tighter about me. My body vibrates and ripples in the currents but I haven't the power to push my way up. The sun, that star, narrows itself to saucer, shilling, dot, gone. I cannot remember what colour I am and whatever it is these eyes will never see it again. Down here among the bright-headed things, the clacking-jawed things, the white-eyed and pale-blooded things I am flattened by all this weight of water above me and I feel it like a dog sitting on my chest, sleeping its warm body over mine. I feel the end of everything and I feel home.

2

Henry's thoughts rattled around in his head. His head was the same size, but there were half as many thoughts to fill it with. Loose and dry they were, the ones he had left; like gravel and shrivelled beans. Cricket. Tea, and what kind of cake he might eat for it. Rathbone and his marbles; marbles that used to be Henry's and which he lost because he was distracted because half his mind was missing. The hole in his sock. The blister on his ankle from the hole in his sock. Avoiding Mother and that ointment she'll put on his blister if she finds out he has it. Times tables. Always taking the long way home, just in case. Sand in his shoes, rubbing holes in his socks. Touch his shoulder, touch his shoulder, touch his shoulder until Father ties his hand to the chair during dinner so he will stop doing that just for one minute.

He didn't want to draw. One by one, Georgie borrowed his pencils and never gave them back and Henry didn't even mind. Drawing houses, streets, horses, boys: who cares? He held his breath under the bathwater but it wasn't at all the same.

Mother gave him scraps to feed the cat he favoured. He knew she wasn't, but still. Day after day after day he fed her and when she decided it was time she jumped no questions into his lap and turned twice, washed her face, and went to sleep. Her small heart beat against his leg and he knew she wasn't, but still. He watched Wills stumble after her, falling onto his bottom and crying when she escaped his clutches. He saw Father with her, late, when Henry should have been asleep; Father lifted her by the belly and rubbed her torn ears, told her secrets from his day.

They knew his Mark was gone, Mother and Father. Mother washed his back in the bath and she never said a thing. Father was there one day and said, 'Well, well. Maybe she wasn't lying,' and he said it very quietly to himself but Mother heard and asked him, 'Who's lying, George?' and he told her, no one, and it's good that Henry is growing up, he said: he's looking very well.

After that Father took him to the football again and even asked him to play French cricket in the yard. He would walk into the bedroom when Henry was studying and ask him, 'What's that you're reading?' and then want to talk all about the Wars of the Roses or agriculture for hours and hours. 'What do you want to do when you grow up?' he asked Henry, not that he'd ever cared before, and he joked that maybe he should become a butcher like Mr Sidney, and Henry felt a bit of sick rise up in his throat. 'Maybe a sailor,' he said, and Father told him best not, that he'd already had one narrow escape and then he said more, as though he'd meant himself, George, that he'd had a narrow escape, but Henry had heard it in his voice that he'd meant Henry. 'If it's adventure,' he said to Henry, 'or travel you're after, you should try the railways,' but Henry knew the railways in Australia weren't worth a penny.

There was even one horrible afternoon when Father tried to explain to him where babies come from. Henry listened, burning with shame that Father could say those things about Mother, and then he made Georgie wrestle with him until well after dark.

Georgie sat with him sometimes now, in the cupboard. Henry would try to remember the thoughts that had been in his brain, and Georgie would draw, and mostly they would sit quietly but sometimes they would work. For two whole months they collected eggs, just the way Georgie had said, from the tiniest wren to an emu egg Mrs Gallwey had given Henry on his birthday after he'd told her their grand plan. The eggs were lined up on the very top shelf from smallest to largest and every day they would open the cupboard to a richer, danker and more disgusting smell. Henry remembered, almost, what joy felt like. One day they brought the cat into the cupboard with them and she batted the sparrow egg around the shelf until it broke, and they wiped it up as best they could but still that same day Mother said, 'What on earth is that horrific smell?' and before she could investigate further they took the rest of the eggs and hid them behind the laundry where they could rot in peace. 'We'll visit them every day, Henry, won't we?' Georgie asked and Henry said of course they would, and Georgie could draw them and Henry would write notes about what happened. Rats, of course, stole them the very first night and Henry wondered, but only for a moment, what on earth the point of his cat even was.

And sometimes Henry's Uncle William, too, would ask him what he was learning at school, but it was different than the way Father asked. And he would ask, and sometimes Sarah would ask too, if he didn't care so much anymore about the underwater world, and for a while he would ask to see the picture he'd drawn, but when month after month after month went by and nothing changed he thought it would be better to stop. 'Don't show it to me anymore,' he told them, 'not even if I ask.' And he would say, 'Thank you, no, I don't want to draw a picture, but if you'd like we could talk about why it is that the sun makes plants grow.' And Uncle William would tell him all about how sunlight for plants was like food for boys, and they would take the tops of carrots and place them on wet paper and some would be in sunshine and some in shade and one or two they put in the darkest part of the larder, and then they watched and they waited. On the days he wasn't there, Sarah would draw the plants' progress. And when the three of them sat down after tea one evening to write their report on how the sun makes plants grow, Henry tried replacing his old sort of joy with a new sort of joy, and almost got there.

He told Georgie and Mother what he'd learned and Mother told him that he and Georgie could have a part of the garden just to themselves and grow whatever they wanted there, and Georgie and Henry planted beans and sunflowers and lavender that made the bees and butterflies come, and Henry began to think, when his father asked him what he wanted to do when he grew up, that maybe he would live that long and even like it. 'Perhaps a farmer,' he said. 'Or a scientist. Perhaps I could be a botanist and travel to the far corners of the earth collecting plants.' 'Maybe just to the far corners of South Australia,' said his father, 'because you can get there by camel.' And they agreed that camel would be an excellent way to travel and far better than a ship.

3

George was most pleased to find himself cured. Maybe that woman had been Ledwith after all. Or maybe his own damn persistence had got him through this thing. Either way, best not to think back on it; best to just get on.

He should take the family on holiday, he thought, after it had been six months or more without an attack. Henry had been harping on about botany lately: maybe it was time to take the boy on an adventure, set him loose in the bush and see what he came back with. Perhaps they could leave Wills and Georgie with Sarah and just take the oldest boy. Or better yet, why not take the whole family on holiday, Wills, Sarah, William – the lot. If William came they could visit some local pubs.

Speaking of local pubs, wasn't that the neighbour going into one? People said she was some kind of witch. George roused himself from his daydream and paid for the cloth Mr

Barnard had just wrapped for him. *Research,* he told himself as he crossed the road and went into The Rifle Range. He'd never seen a woman drinking in a pub before and you couldn't just let opportunities like that pass you by.

'Missus Gallwey.' George tipped his hat to her then went to the bar and ordered himself a beer. 'Is anyone sitting here?'

'If they are,' she said, 'I can't see them. How can I help you, Mister Hills?'

George sat himself down. 'Lovely afternoon for it, wouldn't you say?'

'I suppose it is.'

'You come here often?'

'Not often,' she said.

'That was quite a storm we had last weekend.'

'Quite. Is there something in particular you wanted to discuss with me, Mister Hills?'

'What do you know about haunting?' he asked.

'Haunting?'

'Or spells. Potions. That sort of thing. Do you know anything about spells to stop a haunting?'

'I'm not really —'

'Or rather, not a spell to stop a haunting, but do you think you can stop a haunting just with the power of your mind? If the haunting isn't a ghost, that is?'

'Well, I suppose it makes a change from the weather or the price of grain. Perhaps you could be a little more specific.

You've been haunted by a ghost that isn't a ghost?'

'I haven't. Not me. There was a fellow in the Sailor's Home a week or two back, said he'd been haunted by a woman —'

'Oh well, that's another thing entirely.'

'No, not like that. Said she was a spirit, he thought, from another plane of existence. Evil, probably. Maybe came direct from hell.'

'Mister Hills, I know this is difficult for many men to fathom, but not every woman will want to have sex with a man just because he fancies her. Sometimes they say no. Saying no doesn't make them a, what did you say? A hell spirit from another plane of existence?'

'Pardon?'

'Men are prone to overreact. They meet a woman, she's beautiful, she talks to them and then they think, oh, she likes me, we'll get married. And she doesn't return the favour, doesn't like him as much as he likes her, so then she's evil, isn't she. She's some kind of hell-spawned bitch to spurn him in this way. And he has dreams where he's tupping her and she laughs at him and then that's it, she's haunting him, she really is a witch. Is that what happened with your … friend, did you say it was?'

'Not a friend. Just a bloke. No, I don't think it was like that at all.'

'It was an actual haunting.'

'Never mind.'

'Mister Hills,' she said. 'I'm not a witch, whatever you might have heard about me. Oh, don't look surprised, of course I know what people say. That I'm a convict, I'm a witch, I'm a whore, I'm a gypsy. You think Neddy doesn't hear things when he's out? Do you think people don't ask him what I get up to, me and Missus Frome both? At least she had the good sense to be a civilised South Australian. There's no redeeming me, filthy New South Welsh that I am, elderly washerwoman with an inexplicable baby.' She tapped her empty glass gently on the bar between them. 'Why don't you fetch me another of these? I've seen some things in my time. Maybe I can help.'

While the publican drew two more beers, George tried to remember how he'd got into this conversation in the first place. He'd been joking, hadn't he? Haunted. He wasn't haunted. He had never been haunted! Guilty conscience was all it was, maybe. For having lewd thoughts. Well, more than thoughts. And the meat, of course. Meat. Could you say, that: meat? Flesh, maybe. He was sorry about that, but then again, no he wasn't. And hadn't Mr Darwin himself said it was the right thing to do? So yes, illness, lingering, perhaps from all the trouble he'd been through. Whatever the doctor said, it must have done some shocking damage to his lungs and heart. A man doesn't just bounce back from that in a matter of months. So illness, lingering. And some guilt. And perhaps wanting to make of that time with Miss Ledwith something that it wasn't. Something other than warm skin and survival. Maybe Gallwey had a point: men did tend to overreact. Whatever it was, had been, it was over now. Done.

He took the beers back.

'Very enlightening, Missus Gallwey,' he said. 'You've given me a great deal to think about.'

'You don't want to tell me more about this haunting your … friend … has been suffering?'

'Ah, it's history now. And as you say, you're not a witch. What possible interest could you have in the dark turnings of a possessed man's mind? None whatsoever. A nice lady like you. Cheers,' he said, and lifted his glass to hers. 'So tell me more about what Missus Frome gets up to.'

Missus Gallwey drained her glass in one impressive draft. 'Thank you, Mister Hills,' she said. 'Now I really must go.'

4

I don't know days. Down here it is just me and the light of a thousand crazy headlamps. Have you seen them? No, you've never been down here. All jaw, they are, and out in front bobs a little lamp. The tiniest fishes, the ones with no brains, can't help their little selves and simply must look, must see, what is it? And they find out it is mostly jaw.

So I watch that. I have watched that. For some long time now that is what I have done: watched that. We call it entertainment. We is me, because there isn't anyone else here. Everyone else here is either food or I am.

This has been a mistake. I could have done nothing much better in the shape of fleet-footed fur.

My eyes are shut down. I have only one shape, soft and tentacled. Everything that was me means nothing at all here, in this freezing trench on an alien world. So instead I live there and then: the once-upon-a-time world that was all ocean, nothing but.

We eat and live and wait. I think.

A mass of flesh drifts down from our sky, a creature softened by death, all the shape gone from it. It hangs above us long enough for me to stop my conversation with myself, wonder at this cloud of fat, lit from inside by a thousand crazy headlamps. It hangs above us long enough for me to forget it's there, and to start the conversation again. This could be there, I say; this could be home. No cloud of fat there, though, was there? I answer. Not that you ever saw, I say, which doesn't mean there wasn't. Were you ever this deep before? I say. I don't answer. I wasn't. But this could be there. I could be there, down deep, where I've never been before. I wouldn't know anyone here. I could be home. I could have slipped. Home, before. And if I could just get a little closer to the sun, that star, I could look and see that all this was just the way it always had been, always was.

The cloud settles to the ocean floor. I am not the first to leave my rocky crack and strip my portion, but for once I am not the last. I coil about it, fill my belly. I eat it and I watch my back, but my tentacles and I are not so tempting when this giant lump of fat sits flaccid and unfighting on the ocean floor. Everyone comes from all around – those crazy headlamps and their friends, cousins and future enemies are all here. Is the world all ocean, nothing but? I throw the thought out there while we're all filling our guts, but no one here knows anything but the deep, cold dark and they can't say if it's all there is because for them it's all there is. They can't say because saying isn't a thing they do.

How do they live like this, without ever knowing day or night or how many times this forsaken planet has turned one face and the other to the sun, that star? This forsaken planet is your planet, I tell myself, but I will not believe it. We have not slipped, I reply; we are at the very bottom of the deepest of deep seas on the rim of a land that is full of tromping uprights with monkey-brain ideas. We will sit here for what will probably be years but who knows and then we will die too and everyone will gather around, charming and chumful the way they are now, and they will eat us until we are gone and then the first and fastest will eat one another until everyone speeds out of there. And that will be the end of this story, which may as well already be ended because what is there down here but dark and cold and the occasional floating lump of rancid fat? And while we, while I, am down here rotting, up there they will wrap themselves in metal and go to my home and kill everything that's mine. And whoever I am then and there will flee back here and all of this will start again.

We eat. I eat. I crawl back to my dark cavern to slowly die. I returned here to this wet somewhat home and I have found that all the loneliness there has ever been waits here still.

You should get up there and look. Up there near the sun, that star. Go up. Look. Listen. You're full of wet fat now. You will never be this unhungry again. Living on scraps of grim white-eyed bone monster? That won't do it. This is it. Now.

You understand you have to come too, I remind myself. Well, I hadn't. But I do now. And I still think we should.

And not right then but soon after, when this ocean floor is settled, when all of the fat is gone and the bigger of the things with teeth dispersed, when we've remembered that yes it is possible to be even lonelier than you are when you are feeding on wet, rotten fat with the cousins of some crazy lantern heads, then. When we remember that it is one thing to be in a world all ocean when that world is your own and quite another to be in a world all ocean when no one down there gives a holy damn about you and the only one who does on the whole bereft and stinking planet is some skinny-legged filthy-fingered swollen-hearted little upright on some dusty island up there where the sun is hot and the air is dry, well: then. That's when we go. Then.

That is when I go.

I cling. I slide, crawl and climb and I cling. I rest, rest, rest, rest. I slide. I stop. I jet and swim, swim, swim, swim. I stop and cling and for an hour a day a week I hide and shrink in terror. I check and check and check and slide and then I jet and then I swim.

And there it is, its tiny dot in the corner of my eye which

turns out to be that warm, beautiful life-giver, the sun. That star. The sun. It is dot, it is shilling, it is saucer and then here it is in my eyes and ears, and all around me the breaking of the ocean on the shore.

Just me, here, on this world that maybe once was but certainly isn't now all ocean, and I am filling my eyes with ships and boats and people and jetties and even look a horse there and a man and yes, it is: I am right back where I started.

You should go find Henry, I tell myself, and then I remember that I don't have anyone to talk to anymore and if I want someone to talk to ever again, that's exactly what I should do.

SOME JOURNEYS

1

'Put your head … just put your head through … oh goddamn it.'

The shirt had torn. It was Ivan's last shirt and it had torn nearly in half and there wasn't another one to replace it. His arms didn't fit his sleeves anymore. He kept changing shape in inexplicable ways. He wanted new things, like food he could chew and to walk around.

'Can I put this thing in some kind of harness and hang it from a wall?' Beatrice asked Mrs Frome, who was half-heartedly pulling weeds from the gaps between the courtyard cobblestones. 'Not all day, you understand. But for a good portion.'

'You tell me, love,' Mrs Frome replied. 'I've never had the misfortune. Did you try it with your own baby?'

'I can hardly remember yesterday, don't ask me to remember twenty, fifty, a thousand years or whatever it's been.' Bea rummaged through her own clothes until she found a camisole small enough to look like a pinafore for the child and slipped it over his head. 'I have to get this baby some clothes.'

'Well, he's not really a baby anymore, is he? Which I suppose is the problem.'

'One of the problems. Can you watch him for me while I go down to Military Road?'

Mrs Frome nodded, which Bea assumed meant yes she'd be in the vicinity but no she didn't make any promises about actually watching, which was good enough for now.

As she nursed a small glass of beer in the back bar of the pub, Bea wondered how terrible it would be of her to buy a ticket on the next steamer back to Sydney and just leave the boy here. She hadn't wanted him or asked for him. She was fond of him, but she wouldn't say she loved him, as such. It wasn't that she wished him ill or even that she had anything in particular to do that she couldn't do with Ivan around. But after all those long years of putting up with a husband she couldn't abide, she had no inclination to spend what was left with someone else's uninteresting child. Better loneliness, she thought. At least loneliness gave a woman time to think.

Oh but what about the poor child? How would he feel, abandoned first by his mother and then by his grandmother? What great weight of sorrow mightn't the unfortunate sod lug through life? Could she really condemn him to live the life of an Oliver Twist, a David Copperfield, an impoverished, neglected orphan thrown into a life of crime and despair? But ah, she reminded herself, it all turned out fine in the end, didn't it? Twist and Copperfield both ended up comfortable children, well-off men. And happy, too. Though of course that was thanks to their mysterious relatives appearing out of nowhere and spiriting them off to a new life. Bea was Ivan's mysterious relative. And Bea was tired of spiriting.

She chanced her luck and ordered another beer. The barman complied.

She had no great ambition for her life, but she did have a little. Forty-five years old and many might say that was it, not much left that an old dried-up widow like her could hope for. But her body still worked fine, head to toe and everything round the middle section as well. She could dance. She could drink. Men were happy to come to her bed and maybe one day she'd find one she liked for more than a day or two at a time. She would like to see what else life had to offer. Work a little harder and make a bit more money, then spend it on a passage to San Francisco, New York, maybe Italy or Jordan or Zanzibar. The Spice Islands. All that was possible with a child, of course, but why would anyone intentionally take an unwanted guest with them on a journey of adventure? You wouldn't see some man invite his ancient aunty along for the ride as he cavorted off to New Guinea. He'd go alone, or with someone whose company he actually enjoyed. Why shouldn't she – as capable of drinking a beer as any man, as capable of managing herself on an ocean voyage, of mastering her own feelings, of earning her own passage – do the same?

She emphasised the point by ordering herself a third beer, which she drank at speed. On Military Road the tedium of shopping for miniature shirts and trousers was much relieved by the light buzzing in her head and thrilling of her skin, and so with time to spare she bought a little trinket for Mrs Frome as well.

'What's all this then?' Mrs Frome asked as Beatrice plunked the package down on the kitchen table.

'You can easily answer that question yourself by unwrapping it,' she replied. 'Is Ivan still in the yard?'

'I suppose so,' Mrs Frome said from the depths of the larder.

Ivan had fallen asleep with his bottom in a puddle, which would have been a problem had he been wearing any clothes. As it was, Bea dried him off and wondered if really there was any point at all dressing a person with so little sense of self-preservation. Though if she was honest with herself, given the chance she'd much rather lounge about stark naked. And so she decided to let him be for the remainder of the day. The weather was warm. And besides, if she was going to leave him at an orphanage, then he would probably never get the chance to run naked again.

Was she really going to leave him at an orphanage? A good orphanage, mind you. Not one of those orphanages where they send the children to work in factories and starve them and beat them. The kind where they feed them properly and they have a comfortable bed and warm clothes and where they get an education. That kind. She should probably wait until she sobered up before she decided, but deep down she thought that yes, she probably would. That big building on the beach at Largs – wasn't that an orphanage?

'Come here, Ivan,' she called into the courtyard from her bed in the stable. 'Ivan, are you out there?' Ivan!' And after a few more tries the child tottered in. She sat him on the bed next to her. He wasn't a bad boy. Nice-looking, funny. 'Where's Mama?' she asked him, and preoccupied with a strip of rabbit skin he'd found somewhere, he waved one hand absently and said, 'Gone'.

'And Papa?'

'Gone.'

She watched to see if he cried or even scrunched his little face up as though he was having sad thoughts, but there was none of that.

'Ribbit?' he asked.

'Rabbit,' she told him. 'It's fur from a rabbit.'

'Mumum,' he said, even though she kept telling him not to call her that, 'the ribbit's gone?'

'Somewhat,' she said. 'The rabbit's fur is here, but most of the rabbit is gone. Yes. Rabbit gone.'

'Where's the ribbit?'

'Gone.'

He fondled the fur a little longer.

'Where's the ribbit?'

'The rabbit's gone.'

'Gone?'

She nodded.

He tucked the piece of fur into the pocket of her shirt.

'Mumum, the ribbit's gone.'

'That's right,' she said.

He pulled it out again.

'Ribbit!' and he squealed with glee and bounced on the bed. 'Mumum, ribbit, ribbit, ribbit, ribbit!'

'Yes, it's a rabbit. Do you want to take your rabbit outside?'

He tucked the fur into her pocket.

'Ribbit's gone.'

She had nothing to add.

'Mumum, ribbit's gone.'

He stared at her.

'MUMUM, ribbit's gone!'

'Yes, the rabbit is gone.'

He pulled the fur from her pocket and squealed again, louder than before. 'RIBBIT! Ribbit, ribbit, ribbit, ribbit, ribbit!' and bounced on the bed until he fell over and banged his elbow and started to wail.

She picked him up and rubbed the sore spot until he calmed down, dabbed a little ointment on it to reassure him something was being done, then tucked him into the bed thinking she'd lie quietly beside him for a few moments until the temperature cooled down outside. He fell asleep immediately and, as he always did, stretched his little limbs into every corner of the small bed, smushing his heels into her kidneys and forcing her back to her feet.

Outside she rolled herself a cigarette and listened to the houses around her. She could hear that boy Henry telling his mother about volcanoes in excruciating detail and his little brother chiming in with outright fictions about a giant volcano from the sea that will swallow them all. From an upstairs window, Bea heard the shrieks of a furious toddler. The little girl who lived next door to them was reciting her times tables and getting most of them wrong. Bea exhaled smoke and watched it curl up to the pink and orange clouds above the little colony of South Australia, where no one was of convict stock and everyone went to church and life was lovely and calm and polite. She yelped and dropped the butt, which had burned her finger. 'Hang this,' she said.

Mrs Frome was stirring some kind of stew when Bea went into the kitchen.

'Don't you ever want to live somewhere else?' she asked, taking over the chopping of carrots so Mrs Frome could rest her buniony old feet.

'What do you mean, darl? The only other place I'm likely to live is the hospital, and not for very long at that.'

Mrs Frome was all of fifty-five, but she'd been in this house since her father died and left it to her thirty years ago.

'You never wanted to go somewhere? To travel? Even to the mother country?'

'England? Bloody damp in England. All grey and everyone in their grey suits muttering about the rain is what I've heard. Why would you leave all this for that?'

Mrs Frome was a strong advocate of the young colony, a lover of the wind off the ocean, the new museum, the jetty at Semaphore, raucous dances in the run-down blocks where the itinerant sailors lived. She'd been known to fraternise with the local tribe in the park in town, sharing a little fire-cooked meat – anyone who sang and could teach her a song was someone Mrs Frome thought worth spending time with.

'I'd never waste my time with England. Stuck-up, they are.'

'South America, then. The Argentine. Cowboys and pampas and ancient pyramids and mystical jungles.'

'I expect that's Egypt you're thinking of. I've no time for any of that. Disease-ridden fleshpots, those places, uncivilised savages with over-spiced food and no notion of how to make a decent cup of tea.'

'I hear the tea is good in India.'

'No, no – I'm South Australian born and raised, I'll live and die here and nowhere else. God's country. Speaking of tea …'

Bea added the last of the vegetables to the stew and put a pot of tea on, then sat down at the kitchen table too.

'So you've got itchy feet, do you, lassie?' Mrs Frome asked.

'I don't know,' said Beatrice, and she didn't know. She remembered why she'd come to South Australia in the first place, to dump the child on her younger sister, and wondered if that was still a remote possibility. There'd been a letter or three between them since her sister's husband had died. Anne-Marie, the sister, had gone to live with her husband's elder brother and his family until the lack of space became too much for them all. Then came the great good fortune that the younger brother had taken a shine to her and was happy to marry her and the whole bunch of them, given they were as close to being his children as a man could hope without being the natural father. Anne-Marie never mentioned her feelings on the matter – whether the brother was an appealing prospect not just as a safe harbour but also as a man. But when circumstances are straitened, Bea supposed, best not to put too much importance on that kind of thing. Since the marriage, which had been a small affair and Bea informed that it probably wasn't worth her while making the trip, correspondence had dried up. Now and again she thought of making the journey up through the hills to the German village. Action had not yet followed inclination. Would it be worth some exploratory questions to see whether Anne-Marie could inconspicuously add another to the brood?

'Well, as you're so forthcoming, maybe we should just eat our dinner in silence,' Mrs Frome said.

'I'm sorry.' Beatrice tried to look attentive. 'Would you like me to serve the stew?'

'Oh, if it's not too much bother, dearie,' Mrs Frome said, easing herself back into her chair and raising her feet again on her tattered footstool, embroidered with a dachshund gnawing at its own tail.

She could visit the orphanage. Just to see. And maybe send a letter to her sister. When dinner was done and Mrs Frome napping in her armchair, Bea scratched a little something out.

'Dear Anne-Marie, If you are properly settled now, Ivan and I would like to take an opportunity to visit you. I cannot remember if I told you about Ivan – he is my grandson, left with me by my daughter before I came to South Australia. Please let us know when it might be convenient to visit, and whether we might stay a night or two. Your sister, Beatrice.'

2

It was a black joke the day George had squatted, breathless yet again, oh yes, that old thing once more, his back against a wall down a side alley just off the esplanade, his guts choking him, his eyes spotted blind, his heart a monster in his chest that fought the ribs holding it as though it would tear itself free and flop dead on the ground before him. He'd been nearly a year out of this. He was free! He thought he was free. He propped himself against that wall down a side alley looking for all the world like a washed-up drunk or a shattered old man. A black joke that, unappealing as he must have seemed, he was unerringly targeted by a frantic sailor, tugging at his coat sleeve and urging him please sir, please sir, you must come, you must help.

Help who, what, how, when all around him dizziness swirled and his throat clamped shut and he could feel a thrill of electricity up and down each hair on the skin of his arms. *Leave me, man,* he wanted to yell, *I am dying and just want to be left alone to die.* But his vision narrowed down to the dimmest of pinpricks, his voice broken to pieces by his trembling heart, he could not manage even a single word.

Instead he struggled to his feet and swallowed back the vomit that rose in him as the earth tipped and yawed, pulled on by this limping, scatter-witted man at his elbow.

'Hurry sir, hurry.'

'What is it?' George managed to breathe out, and the man told him a boat, sir, a ship, run aground, more than a hundred aboard but how will we save them, sir? And George nearly fell to the ground laughing but that he knew only a crazy man would find a terrible wreck the world's most hilarious joke.

There is nowhere here a ship could run aground, he wanted to tell the man, but the urgency in his voice pulled George on though as he looked about him he did not see the running crowds you'd expect at a tragedy of that size.

'There,' the man told him, and pointed towards the horizon. Dry land all the way, it was, and buildings, carriages, shops, homes, hotels. 'There! Can't you see? Do you need my glass, sir?' and the man began fumbling in the filthy bag slung over his shoulder. Finding nothing he abandoned the search. 'There! Eight days it has foundered and almost all aboard are dead.'

'Eight days, you say. Food? Do they have food?' George muttered. 'Water? Do they have water?'

'Nothing! They have nothing! Eight days in this freezing wind!' he howled, as the harsh sun of late summer burned down upon both their heads. 'This freezing wind! How will they live? Their poor, damned souls!'

George grabbed the man and shook him until he stopped screeching, shook him until he dropped the bag, shook him until he began to whimper and when he was weeping openly he threw him to the cobblestones and kicked him once for good measure. 'Why don't you send the fucking lifeboat, you heartless prick?' he hissed into the man's purpled face, and then he turned and strode away.

It felt better. It felt a hundred, thousand, million times better. His chest swelled, his lungs full of air for the first time in ten years or maybe a lifetime. A grin spread across his face and he filled that grin with one whisky then another, until he settled enough to turn to beer. When the beer had done God's good work he washed his hands, smoothed his hair and turned his face to home.

'Come with me, boy,' he said to Henry, who was hunched over another of his drawings in a corner of his room. 'Now!'

He took the boy's hand and marched him downstairs, where he slammed open the backstairs cupboard door. 'Let's take a look at what we have in here.'

Jars – pickling jars, preserving jars – full, half-full, one-third-full – with bubbling, lumpy liquids in greys and greens and, once, an acid pink. 'Fetch a box, boy. Be smart about it,' he said, and when Henry was not back within the minute yelled after him, 'from the larder. There are boxes in the larder.' Another jar of flaked, reddish-brown skin. Apple cores in all states of disintegration.

'Put them all in there,' he said, and when Henry stood shocked, 'the jars. Put them in the box. Then take them to the laundry and clean each of them until they shine and then you can return them to your mother's kitchen where they belong.' He pulled the boy's shirt collar down. 'That filthy thing's back again, I see. Maybe I should slice it off. Take it off with a knife.' He gripped a little harder. 'This has all gone too far, Henry. All of it. You. You need to behave like a normal boy. You need to think like a normal boy. What's this?' Something's skeleton, small; not human, thankfully. 'You're killing things now? Saving their corpses?'

'The cat killed it. Years ago.'

'The cat did it, did she? But you thought you'd keep the rotting corpse in a cupboard inside the house? Well, you won't be needing it anymore,' and he dropped the skeleton to the floor and crushed it with his boot. 'Fetch the broom and clean all this out, then wash those jars like I told you. Your mother and I will think about what to do with you.'

Where was the boy's mother?

'Georgie –' his second son was daydreaming as always, sitting on the hallway floor and staring out the window when he was supposed to be polishing the family's shoes – 'where's your mother?'

Georgie scratched his forehead with the polishing rag, leaving a black smear across his eyebrow. 'Shopping? Maybe she went shopping with Aunty Sarah?'

'Well, get on with cleaning those shoes. And don't play with your brother anymore.'

'Wills?'

'No, not Wills. Henry. I don't want you playing with Henry. He's a bad influence.'

George could feel a headache creeping up on him. He cut himself a slice of bread. That wasn't enough so he cut a chunk of cheddar, too. He sat on the back steps chewing away at them, listening to the clink of jars in the laundry and squinting at the sun. There was a power in him, he felt it now. All this pain, all this fear: he was coming through to the other side of it. Whatever eggs had been laid inside him on Carpenters Reef, they were beginning to hatch. He had been equal to it. He had never turned his back on it. He was starting to see what it had all meant.

He heard the front door open and the voices of Eliza, Sarah, William.

'William!' he yelled up the hallway. 'Just the man I want to see.'

'George,' Eliza said as he hunted them down in the kitchen, 'you're tracking dirt in on your boots. Can you leave them inside the back door?'

He ignored her. 'William,' he said. 'I need to talk to you. Outside.'

'George, what's going on?' Eliza would not stop. 'What happened to the cupboard?'

'I'll tell you later. Tend to the child, will you.' Wills was coughing and had gone quite red in the face. 'William?'

'Excuse me, ladies,' William said, tediously cleaning his hands on a napkin. 'What is it, George?'

He'd already told the man they needed to talk outside, so he took his dirty boots back out there to wait.

'Not near the laundry,' he said, when William eventually made his way out. 'In fact, let's walk. We can go to The Rifle Range. We won't know anyone there.'

'George, can you tell me what this is about? Sarah and I were just about to head home.'

'Well, tell Sarah you'll meet her there. It's important.'

'Have you been drinking already?'

'Most likely. Go on, let her know – I'll meet you out the front.'

Come on, man. Come on. George kicked his toes against the front wall and waited under the sweating sun. That infernal hot wind was picking up again, driving grit between his teeth. No place for a civilised man, Port Adelaide in the summer. Should all learn from the natives. Strip off. Get in the river. Sleep under a tree till the worst of it passes. Perhaps he'd take another trip into town and have a bath in that lily pond.

'Finally.'

William's ridiculous straw hat blew off the second he stepped out the front door and George enjoyed watching him chase it for a moment down the road.

'Got your hat?' he asked, laughing.

'George, really. What's all this about?'

'Walk, walk.' They walked in silence until the corner of the street, then, 'You remember Bridget Ledwith?' he asked.

'I beg your pardon?'

'Bridget Ledwith. From the ship.'

'The ship?'

'The *Admella*, William. This isn't very hard for a man of your learning. The *Admella*.'

'Oh. Yes, the woman survivor. I know who you mean.'

'You told me once to keep away from her.'

'I did?'

'You did. Back when I was still sailing. Before I married Eliza. You warned me away from her. Not in so many words. Marry Eliza, you said. Stop searching. You didn't say it like that, but you warned me.'

'George, what's going on? Are you all right? How *much* have you been drinking?' William had stopped walking again.

'It was good advice, I'm not angry. Keep up, William. I don't know how much you really knew about us, about Bridget and me. Keep walking! We'll get you out of this heat soon, put a beer inside you.' He took his brother-in-law's arm. 'Feeling faint, are you? Need a bathchair, perhaps?' William didn't reply. 'Whatever it was you knew, it doesn't matter now. The thing is, she's a witch, I'm sure of it. Some kind of witch. Or maybe a succubus or a siren. Not a real woman. Not a human woman. It explains how she appeared on board the boat – I told you about that, didn't I? She wasn't there when we left Port, William – I'm sure I've told you. She appeared, among the horses, like some wraith. And then after we sank, she was there with me, the whole time, on the wreck. Naked. Wrapped herself around me, she did. She's the reason I lived. I should have died – at least, that's what I thought until today. That I should have died. I didn't die because of her. She warmed me with whatever hellfire sustained her own breath. And she fed me human meat. Oh, don't look at me like that, you know we were cannibals. You've never left me alone about it. And all this time I've been tearing myself apart over it, why did I live, I should have died. I've been physically sick every day of my life with the self-loathing of it. But that's changed now, William. It's changed. I see it now. Chin up, man, get in here and I'll buy you an ale.'

He left William sweating at a table and fetched two beers. 'You follow me so far, don't you?'

'George, did you fall down? Have you hurt your head?'

'Drink up, William, you don't look well. Stop fretting

and have a drink. I'm telling you I'm fine now. I was so, so
unwell before. I've been unwell for so long. But not now. Did
I tell you I've been hunting her? You know she disappeared?
Of course you do, that's right. You told me to stop hunting
her. I didn't though, William. I did marry Eliza, you know
that. But I didn't stop. You see, I saw her the day Henry was
born. Sarah knows, she'll tell you. Bridget was there, when
Henry was born … what? What is it?'

'What do you mean, Sarah knows?'

'Sarah knows, about the midwife. She was there with the
midwife. Ledwith, the midwife was Bridget Ledwith. She
didn't look like her, she wore a disguise, but it was her. But
then she disappeared again and I almost gave up. You see,
William, I had to find her because I was convinced she'd
cursed me somehow, taken away my humanity, destroyed
me with an illness that stole my breath and my sleep and
my mind. I was going to find her and kill her so I could
be a normal man again, William, like you. Well, maybe not
like you. No, I'm just joking, brother – you're a good man.
Another?'

William was a terribly slow drinker. George finished the
last of his brother's glass and got them two more.

'The thing is, though,' he said, as he put the glasses on
the table, 'I've realised now that whatever this is she did to
me, it's a blessing, not a curse. Oh, I'm pretty sure she meant
it as a curse but through my strength and my perseverance

I've changed its form. What was it you were telling the boys about sandstone and limestone the other night?'

'When you put sandstone under pressure it becomes limestone. I don't see how this —'

'Exactly! She gave me a pale, crumbly curse and with the pressure of my forbearance I've turned it into a pure, white, strong blessing. Exactly! I thought I'd found her, you know, a few years back.' He dropped his voice. 'Met her in the gardens. All arranged by letter. Gorgeous, she was. It wasn't Ledwith. Turned out it was some showgirl, running a confidence trick, passing herself off as Ledwith. Gorgeous, though. Spicy character. She wanted me to come back to her place. Said you could come along too. If you ever get the urge, let me know, I have her address.'

'Please, just stop talking for a moment. Can you stop?'

'This is the important bit. I'm nearly finished. What I've realised is that whatever it was she did to me on the *Admella*, it's become a power now, a strength. I don't understand yet what it's for, but I can feel it inside me. And I know the first thing I need to do. I have to fix Henry. I need your advice – how do I fix Henry? Wait, wait –' George held up his hand – 'I just have to make sure you understand. She was there, at his birth. She gave him that birthmark, that thing on his back, I'm sure of it. And it twisted him inside, he has some part of her evil oceanic wickedness inside him. The mark went, but not the evil, not the evil.' He suddenly remembered: the mark was back. No surprises there. You can't erase wickedness that easily. It had to go. The mark had to go or the boy had to go. 'You saw what he had in that cupboard? Bodies, corpses. Festering jars of muck. And those things he draws. He's not normal. He's not a normal boy. We need to fix him, William. The women can't do it. Eliza can't do it, she doesn't even see it. She thinks he's sweet. She doesn't know anything about what the world is like. But you and I do. I've seen terrible things. You've read terrible things. Tell me what to do. Wait, I'll get more beer.'

3

He had to go. They had to go. Over and over and over in his head the voice saying go go go go go go go.

To California? I can't, he kept saying. I can't go there, I can't take you there.

You want your father to slice you open with a knife? He's out now, he's gone out now, but he's coming back and he's already told you, he's going to slice you open with a knife. We have to go.

I don't even know where! I don't know where to go – you still want to find this man? This shade? I don't ever remember his name, Mark; that was so long ago. I don't know where he lives, I don't know anything. I don't have any money!

Ask that woman. Find him. We have to go.

Why don't you just go? Henry said. Why don't you go and leave me like you left me before? Why did you even come back if you're just going to go again?

He had felt the cool ooze of her mind back into his in the middle of a fierce summer storm, Georgie sleeping as Henry lay with the covers thrown off, watching lightning crack open the sky. Her sandy skin slipped across his, the clutch of it firm and Henry felt pulled back together again, sound, all of him back inside himself where it belonged.

Henry had remembered the French cricket, the help with homework, the football matches, his father's hand proud upon his back.

And he had remembered the dry rustle of his lonely thoughts and the world shrunk small and knowing that it wasn't him, that boy playing cricket in the backyard, that boy who Father boasted of to his friends.

He probably should have peeled her off, dropped her out the window to the street below and carried on as a proper, normal boy, blithely happy in a world of a marbles, pies and playground beatings. But he had not. Mark knew that and Mark knew why and Mark and Henry both knew that if either of them was leaving they both were.

So Henry made plans for the two of them to leave. He crept under the parlour window. Mother, Aunty Sarah, talking about babies. He pressed his ear against the back door. No Father.

He crept in, upstairs, into his and Georgie's bedroom. He pulled his schoolbag from the cupboard, packed a jumper, his book about volcanoes, the rock candy that said 'Glenelg' all the way through from end to end, one more shirt. He needed apples and pie from the kitchen.

'Are you going somewhere?' Georgie called to him from the hallway, where he was still half-heartedly polishing shoes.

'Shhh!'

Georgie put the shoe down and gripped for a moment at his belly. 'Ow,' he said. He leaned back against the wall rubbing at his belly button.

'Is it your tummy still?' Henry asked him, but Georgie shook his head, said it was nothing. He unfolded himself and came into the kitchen, asked again, 'Where are you going?'

'Just to Missus Gallwey's for a minute.'

'Why do you need your schoolbag?'

'I'm going to hide it there in case I ever need to run away.' Henry didn't want to say he was going now, he didn't know if he was going now, he had no money and nowhere to go.

'You should tell me if you're going to run away, in case I want to come too.'

Henry nodded.

'You shouldn't hide pie at Missus Gallwey's,' Georgie said. 'It'll rot before you're ready to go. Then your clothes will smell terrible.'

Henry looked at the pie in his hand. 'This is for now,' he said, and he broke a chunk off for Georgie.

'I'll come with you. I'm sick of polishing.'

He needed to talk to Mrs Gallwey. He needed to find

out the man's name, the man with the mark, the shade. He
needed to know where, exactly, he lived. He needed ideas
about how to get there. Georgie couldn't hear any of that.

'Aren't you sick?' he said. For days, Georgie had been
complaining about his swollen, aching belly.

'Maybe? It doesn't hurt much right now. I could come.'

'No, wait here,' he said. 'I need you to create a diversion
if Father comes back.'

'A what?'

'He'll want to know where I am. Make up a story. Or
confuse him. Ask him a lot of questions about bookkeeping
or the best way to lay a fire.'

Georgie laughed. 'I can do that. Don't go for too long!'

But Mrs Gallwey wasn't there. Gone up to the Hills, Mrs
Frome told him. Away a few days, visiting her sister. Could
she help? But she couldn't.

He would hide at the creek for a while. Camp. Wait.
Think. Hide.

Georgie stuck his head over the wall. 'What are you doing?'

'I might go to the creek.' Georgie loved the creek. Henry
scrambled around in his brain, his brains, for more. 'But
maybe I won't. I heard there's a tramp down there. Dangerous.
Eats children.'

'Does he have a treasure? I heard he has a treasure.'

'What do you mean you heard? You never heard anything
about it.'

'I did too. I was at the butcher with Mother and she was talking to Missus Callan and it was *so* boring and I was over in the corner trying to see the lizard that sometimes crawls out from behind the meat safe and I heard Daniel Hoffman taking to Ian Callan and he was saying there was a tramp at the creek and he had a treasure.'

Really? Maybe there was a tramp.

'All right, come with me.' It would be less lonely if Georgie came too.

They took back streets and alleyways, a small hill stiff with scrub, over and down until they stood on the edge of the creek. The creek was really a drain, brick-lined and full of rubbish that washed down whenever there was a flood. They found a dim, quiet place in the trees alongside, somewhere the mud wasn't too sticky, and ate the rest of the pie.

'So where does the tramp live?' Georgie asked, and Henry reached over to wipe the crumbs off his chin. 'Are we going to go find him?'

'He lives …' Henry went closer to the water, squinted his eyes and looked off along the drain.

'What? I can't hear you, you're facing away from me. You should turn around when you talk to someone.'

'What do you mean, what?' Henry turned around. 'Oh for God's sake – come down here where you can see.' Georgie slid down the slope and looked where Henry was pointing. 'He lives over there. Oh, you can't see from here. Follow me.'

He strode off, then turned back to check where Georgie was. 'Follow me – but you have to be quiet!'

'I'm good at being quiet,' Georgie said quietly. 'You know that, Henry.'

Henry had to admit it was true. Even now that he was big, Georgie would hide in the tiniest places, could play alone for hours, could draw pictures in a corner of the laundry until dark and didn't need Henry or anyone else.

But Henry didn't say that.

He crept closer to the bank of the drain. Georgie would be behind him, he knew. No need to look back: Georgie followed instructions well.

'Over there.' Henry pointed to the low bridge.

'It's the bridge.'

'I know it's the bridge. That's where he lives.'

'On the bridge? Henry, we walk across that bridge all the time. We would have seen him.'

'*Under* the bridge. He lives under the bridge. Look, where it's dark. See the bush that hangs down in the water? Behind there.'

Henry tried to remember what he'd heard at school when he was young and stupid like Ian Callan. He'd heard a killer lived there. He killed blackfellas and swaggies, everyone said. He killed them and drained out their blood to make a potion, then hid their bodies in the weeds on the edges of town. Mr Sidney had shown him one once.

'Remember, this is a secret.'

'I remember, Henry.'

He didn't know what he'd do if they did find the tramp. He probably wasn't even here. And if he was here?

He probably wasn't even here. Henry reminded himself he was here to run away from home, not to look for any tramp, but then he remembered what Georgie had heard about the treasure. Even though it was probably all lies, he couldn't help hoping. With a treasure, he could take a ship to California.

'And don't forget, he has a treasure. We have to get his treasure,' Henry said.

'I *know* he has a treasure. Isn't that why we're here? For the treasure?'

'Yes. We're here for the treasure. So maybe it's even better if the tramp has gone. Then we can look for the treasure without defeating the tramp first.'

'How will we defeat him if he's there?'

'I don't think he'll be there.'

'What if he is there? Won't he be stronger than us?' Georgie was still speaking very quietly.

'I'm strong, and you can trick him. We'll trick him into giving us the treasure.'

'I know some tricks.'

They took each step slowly, Henry lifting his feet higher than usual to show Georgie how important it was to be quiet, to be careful. As they got closer to the bridge, Henry crouched behind sparse shrubs, peering between them, making sure they hadn't been spotted yet. Nothing much moved down there; just the water. The slimy stones of the bridge dripped.

'Is that him?' Georgie's voice was even quieter now.

'What? Is what him?' Henry tried to be just as quiet, but failed. 'Where?'

'Where the bushes moved. See?' Georgie edged his way forward, quicker than Henry liked. Henry crawled behind him, but Georgie was faster.

Georgie looked back towards him, then pointed again at the bushes, raising his eyebrows.

Henry didn't know if he could see. There were shadows in the water and they moved, a lot, and maybe they were the tramp's boots, swinging, or his hands clutching at cold white fish as they tumbled by in the water.

'I can see his hands.' Henry was firm. Georgie wasn't listening, though; he'd crawled to the bushes near the base of the bridge, on the far side from where the tramp was maybe fishing.

'Georgie, you have to wait for me.' He spoke a little louder. 'Georgie, I'm in charge. This is my treasure, remember?'

Georgie stopped crawling and sat back in the mud, waiting for Henry to catch up.

'You see him?'

'Of course I can see him. He's fishing with his hands.'

Georgie peered into the shadows. 'He is, isn't he! What do we do now, Henry? What's our trick?'

This tramp killed blackfellas. He had a potion. He caught fish in his hands.

'We know where he is now. We'll go home and arm ourselves, and come back tomorrow to overpower him.'

'He might be gone tomorrow. He might leave and take his treasure with him.'

He might take his treasure. Henry stopped to think.

'You should stay and guard him and I'll go home and get weapons,' said Georgie.

'Good idea.' It was a great idea. Henry felt an overpowering love for his brother. Was he really going to go to California and leave Georgie behind? Once he was gone, what would Father do to Georgie? He grabbed Georgie's arm, gripped it tightly for just a second. They needed to go to California together. 'Do you know where my weapons are?' He let go of Georgie's arm.

'Of course. You keep them with your less-favourite skeletons, under the bed.'

Georgie was not supposed to know that. What else did he know? Never mind, it was useful that he knew. Henry would find out more later.

'Good. Then bring ...' Henry thought about what would be best to defeat a treasure-hoarding, potion-brewing tramp.

'Bring the mace, and bring my jousting stick.'

'Which is the maze?'

'The mace. It's the stick with the apple on top, and the apple has nails stuck in it.'

'And the …?'

'The jousting stick is the stick. The big stick. It has string wrapped around at one end that makes a handle. To protect your hand.'

'What's it for?'

'You use it when you ride on a horse, to knock another person over when they're on a horse.'

'Do I need to bring a horse too?'

'Don't be stupid.' Henry couldn't explain why he thought a jousting stick would be best. But he thought if it was what King Arthur had used then it was somehow a little magical, and might be better at defeating tramp magic than an everyday weapon, like an ordinary beating stick. 'Are you sure you don't need me to come back with you? Can you carry them both?'

'Of course I can.'

It would take Georgie a long time to get home, and he would struggle to make his way back carrying the mace and the jousting stick. And he'd been vomiting a bit today; maybe he would vomit in the hall. Mother, or even Father, might catch him and stop him. Georgie would have to lie about why he needed the weapons and where he was going.

But what lie could he tell that would trick them? They might make him reveal Henry's quest. They would come and look for him, and take him home, and then Father would slice him open.

'Hurry now, Georgie. Don't get caught. And if you get caught, death before telling, remember?'

'I remember. I promise, Henry. I'd rather die than tell a secret.'

'Good.'

'Don't let him get away while I'm gone. I'll think of some good tricks, don't worry.' Georgie wasn't quite as quiet now. He was trying to whisper as he snuck away, but it was hard to whisper and sneak.

'Quick! And quiet!'

Georgie smiled over his shoulder and scuttled off among the weeds and out of sight.

Henry sat quietly for a while. He watched some ants, then he followed them a little way into the scrub and found their nest. He poked it with a stick for a while, digging out some of the little white ant grubs. Mrs Gallwey had told him you could eat ant grubs, if you were in the bush and lost and hadn't anything better. Blackfellas ate them, she said, but for choice. They ate them like they were grapes or figs: something sweet for when it wasn't really a mealtime. He offered a grub to his Mark, but Mark was being quiet and still just now. Maybe Mrs Gallwey was eating ant grubs up in the Hills, exploring in the bush. Henry remembered that he was going to be a bush explorer, before he'd realised he had to go to California instead; that he was going to be a bush explorer left with just one camel, all his companions dead and Henry living on just ant grubs and juice he squeezed from the roots of spinifex. You could squeeze juice from spinifex, Henry knew that. He thought maybe spinifex was a plant, because Mrs Gallwey had talked about its roots. Probably just as Henry was about to starve and die he would meet an Afghan. Afghans walked through the desert with camels all loaded up with tools to build the telegraph line. That's what Miss Simpson had told them all at school, that the Afghans had come from Africa with their camels and walked around in the desert and slept at night wrapped up just in a carpet and washed themselves by scrubbing all over with sand. It would be a good life. Perhaps Henry could join up with the Afghans and live on ants and juice from spinifex and sometimes have an apple like that one.

There was an apple floating down the drain, heading for the bridge. Henry hadn't seen the tramp now in ages. Maybe he wasn't even there. Maybe he was out murdering, or had another place, like a blacksmith, where he made his potions. You couldn't make potion under a bridge. You'd need fire to make a potion, surely. The tramp must have gone to his smithy to make a potion and that's why Henry couldn't see him anymore. Maybe he'd taken the fish he caught with his hands, and he was going to cook them on the fire he used to make his potions.

It would be good to eat an apple while he waited.

Henry peered at the bridge for three, four, five seconds. There was nothing there. He came out from the scrub and leaned out over the water to see if he could grab the apple. It wasn't bobbing anymore now. It had caught on something. It actually wasn't a very good apple, it was quite shrivelled. And it had two nails stuck in it.

'Oh, Georgie!' Henry said it out loud, and then he remembered the tramp and ducked back under cover. What if the tramp had heard and was coming for him now? He watched the bridge intently. He lay very, very still. Nothing moved. Nothing moved and nothing moved and nothing moved. He sat up again. The apple was still there. A hungry tramp would have fished the apple out by now, however shrivelled.

Georgie must have dropped the mace in the drain. It had broken, and the apple had floated away.

Georgie did not arrive. Of course he didn't. Why would he come here now when he would worry Henry would yell at him for breaking the mace? He must have gone home, gone back to polish his shoes, knowing Henry would eventually get bored and come home too. Maybe he hoped Henry would never even know about the mace. Georgie might make up some story about how he had been stopped by Mother before he even had a chance to fetch the weapons. That's what Henry would say, if he was in Georgie's place.

He pulled his schoolbag out from under the bush where he'd hidden it. How long could he camp here? Mrs Gallwey wasn't due back from the Hills for days. All the food was gone already. He tried eating an ant grub, but it wasn't very good so he spat it out. He carried his bag down to the water's edge. There was no tramp, and no treasure. He knew that. He walked a little way along the drain in the direction of home, wondering if he could stay the night at Aunty Sarah's. He looked down at the water and saw Georgie, lying in the drain with his eyes wide open and his skin all wrong.

'Georgie?'

Henry slid down into the drain. Georgie's face was under the water and staring up at him.

'Georgie?'

Henry's shoes were all wet and filling up with water and he tugged a bit at Georgie's leg and Georgie just floated a little higher in the drain and stared up at him.

Henry stood there with his feet all wet and waited until he would know what to do.

4

Aunty Sarah sat down beside him on the back steps of the Sailors' Home.

'Do you want to take a walk, Henry? Perhaps we could go to the park?'

'Mother needs me here.'

'Your mother is sleeping now. When she wakes up we can help her.'

'I should help her now. We should do something for her. What can we do for her?'

Sarah put her arm around his shoulders. 'We could make something for everyone's tea.'

'There are so many people here. Who are all these people?' Henry searched in his pocket for a handkerchief and wiped his face. 'When will they all leave?'

'Do you mean your Uncle Hills?'

Henry nodded. Father's brother had arrived at the house

yesterday, two days after Georgie died, with his large, angry wife. Henry did not even know his father had a brother and now Uncle Hills was here in his house, with Aunty Hills, telling Henry what he may and may not do and where to be and at what time.

'I don't know how long he'll be here. But he's helping your father with the Home until your father feels a little better. We have to be patient and helpful and do as he says until then.'

'I wish he would hurry up and feel better.'

'Well, maybe we can help him with that. Come on, let me wipe your face a little more.' Sarah reached for the handkerchief but Henry pulled away, shoving the rag into his pocket and going into the house.

Sarah followed him to the kitchen, where Henry was pulling tins from the pantry shelf, looking for a tray he could use to bake scones. Mrs Abernathy Hills was not far behind. She pushed past Sarah in the corridor.

'What are you doing, boy?' She slapped his hand. 'Leave those things alone. Doesn't your mother have enough to manage without a naughty boy messing up her kitchen?'

Henry glared at her, and deliberately dropped the jug he was holding. Milk and shards of pottery sprayed across the flagstone pantry floor, but Henry did not flinch.

'You terrible, wicked child!' His aunt smacked Henry's face but he stared still at her.

Sarah cried out. 'Missus Hills! Please, we are just trying to make the tea for Henry's mother! The boy is just trying to help!'

'He's a wicked child and he needs to be punished. His mother has been far too lenient with him, and now she is reaping the crop of his evil. Clean this mess up!'

'Are you speaking to me, Missus Hills?' Sarah's voice was cold.

'No, to the boy, of course. Missus Gardiner, I would thank you to watch your tone with me. I am a guest in this house, and the mother of seven boys. I know what boys need. I fear I am far too late for this one, though. He should be put in a home.'

'Missus Hills!' Henry saw Aunty Sarah's eyes get watery, and her voice shook a little. 'Henry is a good boy who loves his mother and father. You should not suggest he has been poorly raised. I have known him since he was born and he is a wonderful child.'

'He is the devil. Look at the fate that has befallen his poor, dear brother. And all because of this wicked, wicked boy. Clean up this mess, boy!'

Henry didn't move, stood with his fists clenched and stared, still, at his mean old aunt who no longer met his eye.

'Henry.' Sarah could not reach him – Mrs Hills's bulk was between them – but she had reached out a hand in his direction. 'Henry, you should go outside. I will clean the kitchen, and then you and I can go for a walk. Please wait for me in the yard. Missus Hills, I would appreciate it if you would let me deal with this myself. I am sure it would not help either George or Eliza to hear us raising our voices at this time. Would you mind?' She firmly pushed Mrs Hills's shoulder.

'I thank you not to touch me, Missus Gardiner.' Mrs Hills had lowered her voice. 'I will leave you alone with this boy, then, if that is what you wish. But you will certainly only make matters worse if you treat him in this soft, indulgent way. My sister-in-law has been too indulgent of him, and she has been taken full advantage of. You mark my words: nothing but evil will come of this child.' She strode out of the room. They could hear her calling down the passageway, 'Mister George Hills, may I remind you again of the necessity of keeping that boy of yours in line. If he is not to become a sheer devil, an alcoholic, a thief, a murderer, you simply must inflict the rod upon him.'

'Henry.' Sarah grasped the boy's hand. 'Henry, don't listen to her. I know I said we must be patient, but your aunt is an awful, awful woman. I cannot tell you not to heed her – she is your aunt – but please do not listen to a word she says. Her mind is bitter and awful. Do you understand? You're a good boy, and we all love you very much.'

Henry did not look up, and let his hand hang slack in his aunt's. When she released her grip, he walked slowly out into the backyard, never once looking at her.

Uncle William found him there, maybe half an hour later,

standing on a box and trying to see into the room where Georgie's body had been laid out.

'Hello, Henry.'

'Hello, Uncle William.'

'Do you want to come inside and see Georgie?'

'What did he die from, Uncle William?'

'Well, the doctor isn't sure, but it seems he drowned.'

Henry got down from the box. William asked him again, 'Do you want to come in with me and see him?'

Henry thought of his experiments, his cats and snakes and lizards. He thought of the headless swaggie Mr Sidney had shown him. Henry knew a lot about death, and the ways it treats a body. He nodded.

The room was dark, the thick drapes drawn and no fire in the grate. The chairs had all been pushed to the side of the room, leaving nothing but a table in the room's centre. On the table there was a small wicker casket, its lid propped open. Flowers were piled around the casket – stinking lilies, making Henry hold his nose. Aunty Sarah was sitting with the body.

'I'm sorry about the mess,' Henry said.

'Pardon?' said William.

'Aunty Sarah, I'm sorry about the mess. I wanted to help.'

'I know you did.' Sarah looked up from her lap. 'We were going to make tea. It doesn't matter now. Maybe tomorrow, after the funeral.'

Henry walked around the table to be further from his Aunt Sarah and peered into the casket. It was dark in this room. He couldn't see much. Georgie looked asleep: pale and sleeping.

'He looks asleep.'

William looked into the casket too. 'He does, doesn't he? He is at peace now.'

'That isn't what dead people look like. Are you sure he's dead?' Henry reached into the casket and touched his brother's hand. He was dead. 'He doesn't look right.'

'Your Aunty Sarah and the nurse have tried to make him look peaceful. It's helpful for your mother and father to see him this way, to think of him sleeping in heaven.'

'It doesn't sound helpful. How will they know that he's dead if he looks like he's sleeping?'

'Well, I think maybe it will take some time for them to get used to the idea that he's gone. This is kinder. They can take some time to get used to never seeing their boy again.'

Henry thought about this. 'Do you think they wish it was me instead?' But he said it very quietly and no one heard. He spoke louder. 'There isn't any way to know, from the outside, how he died.'

William agreed. 'It's true. I think mostly the doctor relies on what he knows of the events leading up to Georgie's death. Georgie was found underwater, so it seems likely he drowned.'

'How do they know I didn't put him there?'

'Henry, don't be silly!' Sarah exclaimed, but William hushed her.

'Well, if you had fought with your brother and pushed him under the water, Georgie would have been bruised. And he wasn't bruised. The doctor thought it looked as though he had fainted, and then fallen in the water.'

'He said he felt sick.'

'So there you are. That is probably what happened.'

'I told him to shut up.'

'Well, you would, wouldn't you? There are few things more annoying than a younger brother complaining about feeling sick.'

'I probably should have helped him instead.'

'But you didn't, because you didn't know he really was sick. And why should you care if he was?' William asked. 'That isn't an older brother's job. An older brother's job is to tease and fight his younger brother, and stick up for him when someone else tries to tease or fight him.'

'Yes, that's my job.' Henry looked into the casket again. 'He was just starting to be a proper boy. Now there's only Wills, and Wills is no use at all. Stupid Georgie, why did he have to drown?' Uncle William sat down and gestured for Henry to sit with him, but Henry didn't want to sit right then, so instead he went out the back door and through the yard and set off towards the water.

Henry had two choices. He could run away to California or he could go to gaol. Father was busy now, comforting Mother and being upset about Georgie, but it couldn't last forever. Sooner or later he would start to ask where Henry was and then he would remember that Henry was a murderer, like Aunty Hills kept saying. He would think about Henry's Mark and he'd either slice him up or he'd send him to gaol.

He hadn't any money to get to California. Could he stow away on a boat? He knew a lot of sailors. Maybe one of the sailors at the Home could help him get to California, and he could find work there or go to the goldfields in Alaska or logging in Oregon. Uncle William had told him how the west coast of America was opening up to civilisation, north to south. He'd shown him on a map. It had been wilderness there, all of it, home to no one but birds and bison and the Red Man, just lying around useless, all that land, until the settlers headed west and found gold and planted crops and built cities and logged the forests and dammed the rivers, and now there was progress. They'd built a new home for humans out of a useless wilderness. Stomping boots, his Mark had said, turning the whole place into dirt, but the anger Henry had felt bubbling up under his skin had been weaker than the urge to go go go.

Stupid Georgie, why did he have to go and die? It was a simple task – get the mace and the jousting stick. That was all he had to do. Fetch the weapons from under the bed and come back, and then they could defeat the tramp and get his treasure.

Maybe he should try to get the tramp's treasure and then he could use it to buy his way to California.

There was no tramp. There was no tramp and there was no treasure and Georgie had gone to get the weapons for no reason at all. Just for a made-up thing in Henry's head.

Henry prised a piece of wood off the edge of the wharf and flung it into the water. He would like to go home and see Mother and have a cuddle and make her a cup of tea. He would like to make Georgie come back.

He would even go to school if that would make his parents happy, and he would sit quietly in class and write properly and learn how to add numbers together and to say a verse in front of the other children. And Mother and Father could be proud of him and he would be allowed to come home.

Maybe he could live with Aunty Sarah and Uncle William. Uncle William didn't think he was a murderer. But what would that be like, to live at their house with no other children and to have to hide whenever Mother and Father came to visit? Perhaps he would have to live always in their attic and never run or climb anymore, just sit and read. Uncle William would visit him in the attic and ask him what he had been reading and tell him facts. That could be good or bad. Uncle William knew some interesting facts. He also knew a great many very dull facts.

He should go back to the house and see if they were waiting for him to take him to gaol.

Had he done anything wrong? He didn't know. He had sent Georgie for the weapons. Georgie wanted to hunt the tramp: he wanted to. Yes, it had been Henry's idea but Henry had been ready to give up and it was Georgie who wanted to get the treasure. But Henry should have known better. Isn't that what Mother was always telling him? That he was almost grown-up now and he should know better. How do you learn how to know better? Henry just did things that were good ideas. Where do the better ideas come from? Were they meant to come from God or something? Then why didn't God ever give them to him? He would like to know better if only someone would help him.

I suppose school is for that, he thought. *They are supposed to teach you to know better.* But who can sit down all day and listen to such boring ideas over and over and over again? Who can do that? They never told him about anything interesting anymore, just adding up numbers over and over again and writing out things from books. The things had already been written once; why write them out again? But whenever he tried to write something new and make the books more interesting he got the cane, and then Father was angry and he and Mother would talk to each other about him and they would always say 'What are we to do about Henry?'

Well, now at least they knew the answer to that. They could send him to gaol. Or slice him to ribbons.

Now it was raining and the wind from the water was horribly cold. The wind was blowing the rain into his face and it hurt his eyes. Could he go home now? He should go home now and if Mother had stopped crying he should make her a cup of tea and blast his horrible Aunty Hills if she got in the way. He should make Mother a cup of tea and give it to her and say, 'Mother, I'm very sorry, I didn't mean to hurt Georgie and I'm sorry that I'm wicked and if you need me to go to gaol I am ready to go.'

That was what he would do.

He pulled another splinter of wood from the pier and dropped it into the water below, watched it eddy and get caught up by the waves and sink. He watched a seagull fight another seagull for a scrap of fish, hopping on one leg even though it clearly had two. He thought about how once he would have tried to lure the seagull to him but how now he knew better than that. He pushed his hands into his pockets and stood up and started walking home.

As he walked he counted stones that were stuck in the gravel of the road. He only counted the shiny ones. If he counted more than ten, his Aunty Hills would be gone when he got back. If he counted more than twenty, Uncle Hills would be gone with her too. If he counted more than thirty, Mother would walk him to gaol and they would cuddle and then Mother would look like she was leaving but instead she would turn around and let him out again. If he counted more than forty, just as he arrived, one of the sailors would be leaving on a trip to California, and he would ask Henry to please come along with him and would tell him that no, he needn't pay his own passage.

If he counted to more than one hundred, his Mark would forget about going to California, and Mother and Father would forgive him and love him even with his Mark and they could all sit down together and talk about what Henry would do at school tomorrow. Then Henry could start all over again and this time he would try his very best to be good.

If he counted to one thousand, Georgie would come back.

He tried to remember how many stones he had seen and realised that he had lost count.

5

Tucked in to bed at Uncle William and Aunty Sarah's house, Henry listened to the murmurings from next door.

'He's lost his mind,' Uncle William said.

'Well, of course he has,' said Aunty Sarah, 'his little boy just drowned. I feel like losing my mind too. He'll get better with time. Or he won't, and we will all learn to live with it.'

'Sarah, it's not grief. Or if it is, it's something else as well. That time, before Georgie – it went clean out of my head with all that's happened – but we'd been shopping with Eliza, remember? Wills had a bit of a cough and Eliza decided we should come back to the house, and when we came back George was there, demanding I go to the pub.'

'Oh, I'd forgotten all that. He was a man possessed, stomping around the house and yelling at the boys, dragging you off to the pub.'

'That's not the half of it. He told me a story – most of it

made no sense at all. Maybe none of it made any sense. It was about the wreck. About that woman, Bridget Ledwith.'

'Bridget who?'

'Ledwith. The woman who survived the wreck. You remember?'

'I think so. Whatever happened to her?'

'There's a question you don't want to go asking George. He has some idea in his head that she kept him alive on the wreck through some form of witchery, that she's some other-worldy creature and that, I guess, he gave her his mortal soul in order to survive. I think that's what he was saying.'

'His what? His *soul*? I didn't think George even knew he had such a thing.'

'He was telling me that he's been having horrible dreams and I think even waking horrors too ever since, all of which he blames on this woman. And he's been trying to find her, to somehow reverse whatever it was that happened to him. He's met some fake Bridget Ledwiths. And he … oh, that's right! He said *you* would know what he was talking about.'

'Me? I barely know what you're talking about.'

'The midwife. He said the midwife at Henry's birth was Bridget Ledwith. And that she had done something horrible to the boy.'

Henry felt sick, even sicker than he'd already felt, which was horribly sick. He swallowed it down and sat very, very still so he could hear the rest. His Mark flickered and writhed and he could feel it listening through his ears.

'She did … she… George didn't even *see* the midwife. He was out getting drunk and by the time he got back Henry was born and the midwife was gone.'

'That's not what he says. He swears he saw her in the house and that Henry's birthmark is some kind of curse she laid on the boy while she was there.'

'He is insane,' said Aunty Sarah.

'I'm glad the boy is here for now. It wasn't safe there for him.'

'Well, it was certainly unpleasant. You think it was actually unsafe? You don't think George would harm him, do you?'

'I couldn't say. But he said that his first mission had to be to "fix Henry". He's obsessed with removing his birthmark. And honestly, I don't see any way such a thing can be done safely, do you?'

'God. He seemed so *nice* when Eliza first met him. The wreck changed him, obviously, but I hadn't realised how profoundly. William, are you sure he said all those things? It wasn't the beer talking?'

'I barely drank. George was doing the drinking for both of us.'

'Well, maybe once he sobered up he realised what nonsense he'd been talking. And all of this, with Georgie …'

It sounded like Aunty Sarah was crying a little. 'Surely that will bring him to his senses?'

'Or drive him further out of them.'

'He's lost one boy – he won't want to lose another.'

'I don't know that he thinks of Henry as his boy. He seems to think he's some creature of this Ledwith woman's.'

'He's a strange boy. But he's not much stranger than you, William.'

'I beg your pardon!'

'I do love him. So much. Almost like he's ours. He's not yours, is he?'

'Madam! What a thing to say about your husband. And about your *sister*!'

Henry was confused. Sarah sounded as though she was laughing now, though, so perhaps it was just a thing adults said. Their voices got quieter, a low hum between them and then some creaking for a while and then it was quiet.

It was me, his Mark told him.

What was you?

It was me. I was her.

You were …?

I was her. The woman. The woman on the wreck, the woman when you were born. It was me.

But you're my Mark! You're mine. You're not a woman.

Henry watched the wreck unfold. He'd seen it before, the horses trying to swim, drowning. He felt terribly sad. The cold of it, but not the pain of cold. Just the fact of cold. A man, his father, young and naked, and Henry always tried to look away at this point but you can't look away when something is inside your mind. And himself, his eyes, in a woman, wet too and naked. They ate a man: he had seen this part before too and he could always taste the taste and it was not horrible like everyone said it would be, it was just cold and wet and for a moment he saw, fleetingly, a great white lump of meat pocked through with tiny bright stars and then it was gone.

Then they were gone, taken away in boats, and Henry saw his father left behind on the wreck and the look on his face oh the look on his face. They were on land and the ground reared up to meet him and his hands fell down beside his feet and a thrill of running soared through him.

You don't need the rest of that, his Mark told him. Too much for you. But here, have this. And there was a baby there, wrinkled, wet and warm and he scampered beside it on tiny feet and spread himself across its back and there they were, baby and Mark, and he could feel his own skin under his own fingers and it was all much, much, much too much and he bashed the back of his head against the wall and cried out and then Sarah was there in the doorway and by his side saying, 'Henry, Henry, Henry, wake up.' He was awake, but he didn't want to open his eyes now or ever again. Sarah held him close and he wished he could be Georgie and be put nice and quiet in the ground after a short and blameless life.

Henry slept and Henry woke and for a moment none of it was there. He tried to remember if today was a day he had to go to school. He wondered if there was a way to get out of it. He remembered his brother was dead and no one cared whether he went to school or not. He remembered his father wanted to remove his Mark with a knife.

In the kitchen he took the bread from the larder and boiled himself an egg. He squashed down thoughts of removing his Mark himself, fed it some egg instead. It was too late anyway. Father hated him. Father thought he was evil. Nothing would fix that. Nothing.

Except maybe this Bridget Ledwith.

Henry tried to shake the thought loose then realised it wasn't his thought, not his to shake.

Like this, and he felt his skin peel away from itself. He gripped his shoulder and recoiled at the unfamiliar humanness. On the floor, he saw a shape that was not a shape, its edges blurred, blending into floor, chair, wall behind. He shook his head but it would not focus, would not turn into sense. He put his hand out to touch, and felt just a faint dampness, a faint scratchiness. He prodded harder and whatever it was resisted his finger. Then a limb wrapped around his arm and sucked itself to him and, suddenly visible, glowed blue-ringed and pulsing.

'Ow!' he screamed, then hushed himself. 'Mark, stop!' The limb retracted and again the floor went shimmery, feverish, furniture and walls wobbling like he was seeing them through the heat of a room on fire. The shape solidified. The shape made a woman and the woman made no sense. A small child's drawing of a mother; a figure seen through sleeplessness and tears.

'What's that supposed to be?' Henry asked, and reached out a hand to touch the familiar skin of his Mark.

'Bridget Ledwith!' the woman slurred at him.

Henry laughed and laughed. 'No, it isn't!'

'It is!'

'Really?'

'Look, it's what your father thinks Bridget Ledwith looks like. Stop laughing!' She was still slurring, and stumbling about like her legs were made of rubber.

'You have to stop!' Henry could barely breathe. 'You have to stop! Aunty Sarah will come down, or Uncle Henry. Oh! Oh goodness, you look so stupid! Oh. Do you want something to eat? Oh, oh never mind, I don't think you could eat without chewing your lip to bits.'

'Henry! I am a witch, a tempshtress. Monster of the sea! All mystery lurks in my skin. I am siren!'

'Really, though. Really. You have to change back. What if Aunty Sarah comes down?'

The Ledwith creature collapsed in on itself, returned to its blobby self, then smeared itself once again over Henry's back.

I can't believe … Henry began to think.

It's true, his Mark told him.

Henry felt a creeping shame for his father. He felt a little bit sorry for him. His fear retreated, two, three steps, when he thought that this, this bizarre apparition, had held his father in thrall for a decade or more. His father was a strange, stumbling human being. His father had no idea either what to think or feel or be.

'Good morning, Henry,' his Aunty Sarah greeted him, and the edge of sadness in her voice reminded him that a whole handful of his guts had been removed. His brother, Georgie, had drowned in a ditch and it was all his own fault. What right had he to be laughing on a sunny morning over a boiled egg when Georgie was just three days in the cold, hard ground? Georgie, who would never see or eat another egg again.

'Could we visit Georgie's grave?' he asked, suddenly overcome with the feeling that he needed to take one, two, twelve, one hundred eggs and lay them over poor little Georgie's poor dead face.

'Of course, if you want to,' she said. 'But you should have some breakfast first.'

'I did that already, Aunty Sarah,' he said, and began to tidy the remains of his meal away.

'Would you like me to make you a cup of tea?' she asked.

'Yes, please,' he said. 'Aunty Sarah? How long can I stay here for?'

'As long as you want, darling. As long as you want. We love having you here.'

'Do you think I should go home?'

'Only if you want to,' she said.

'But what about Mother?' he asked. 'Does Mother need me there?'

He could see her hesitate, search her mind for words. 'Your mother is very, very sad,' she said. 'She needs a lot of time to sleep right now. I'm not sure she really knows what's going on around her …'

'You mean she doesn't really know I'm not there?'

'Darling, I think right now she might not notice if you're not there. But very soon she'll start to notice again, and yes, then she'll need you at home. But perhaps for now, it's better that she only has to care for Wills. It's easier for her not to have to worry about whether you're eating a proper dinner or whether you're going to school. Perhaps it's better if Uncle William and I worry about all of that.'

There was a moment of awkward silence and Henry wondered if he could perhaps grab an apple from the larder and slip out of the house, but he'd left it too late and Aunty Sarah said, 'Shouldn't you be at school?'

'Don't you think I'm too sad to go to school?' he said, and he hoped that Sarah hadn't heard him dying laughing just twenty minutes before. He was sad, though; he really was.

'How about we strike a deal, Henry,' Sarah said. 'You

drink this cup of tea –' she poured it for him – 'and put on your school clothes, and then we'll go visit Georgie's grave, because I think that's a very reasonable request. And once we've finished there I'll walk you to school and explain to the principal why it was you had to be away for a little while. Does that sound fair?'

That did sound fair, and Henry said so.

'Aunty Sarah,' he asked, but then wasn't sure how to continue.

'What is it, dear?'

'Could we … That is, would you … Aunty Sarah, I … did you know about the eggs? About Georgie and the eggs?'

She looked at him kindly, but as though she had no idea what on earth he was on about.

'Georgie loved eggs,' he said. 'He just really did. I don't know why. But there was nothing he loved on earth more than eggs. Chicken eggs. Those tiny eggs left by wrens. We had an emu egg once, Missus Gallwey gave it to us,' and then he remembered he wasn't supposed to see Mrs Gallwey. 'But chicken eggs, those were his everyday, simple favourite.'

Sarah nodded.

'Could we take him an egg?' Henry asked.

'Oh, Henry,' she said, 'we can take him a dozen eggs if you want.' And Aunty Sarah held his face between her hands and kissed his forehead and he felt a long breath squeeze out of him and tears poured out of his eyes. She wrapped him up in her arms and pressed his face against her belly and he cried and cried and cried. And some of it, most of it, was for Georgie, but there was a whole other part of his heart that wept for the Mark he carried on his back and the strangeness of his mind and the way he wished he could just be like every other boy. If he could just be good. If he could only be good.

6

In the little town of Hahndorf, Beatrice had felt herself in one of those rare moments where it was possible to see two futures, one laid over the other. It was simply a matter of taking the tiniest of steps left or right, and one or the other would disappear forever. She had stood for days, utterly immobilised.

Her sister's husband, it turned out, owned a small sausage manufacturer in town, supplying much of the surrounding countryside with traditional German smallgoods. He was doing very well for himself. Anne-Marie was sleek and glorious, her hair shone and the welter of small, sticky hands grabbing at her skirts and her belongings did nothing to erase the soft glow her face had taken on. She had become some kind of maternal saint. Perhaps, Beatrice thought, it was possible to overlook the annoyances of such a boisterous horde of children if one had first, money, and second, a husband as handsome as hers undeniably was. Hector was handsome in face and shape and manner. And so much space – their house sprawled over rooms and rooms, with servants preparing food and then cleaning it all away again.

There was a cottage. Small, Anne-Marie said, but they would love – if Bea wouldn't mind the smallness – for Beatrice and Ivan to live there. It was empty right now: the widow who had lived there, who had managed their sausage store in town, had married a second time and moved to Ironbank. Hector had been looking after the shop. Of course, if Bea would like to look after the shop? Hector would be happy to provide the cottage, already mentioned, and a sizeable allowance. As Anne-Marie's sister she would be welcome to stay as long as she wanted.

Beatrice had sat in the soft armchair by the front window of the cottage and looked out over the Hills. She had thought of all those cousins Ivan would have, to play with and to entertain him. He would come home to the cottage for dinner, and maybe not every night, and he would sleep tight in his bed and then, after breakfast, off he would go again. And Beatrice? She would have all this. This little house to herself. More money than she had ever had. The view of the Hills. People coming and going in the shop.

She would have to behave. She could not bring down shame upon her beautiful glowing sister and her handsome, generous brother-in-law. None of the people – none of the gentlemen – coming and going in the shop could also be coming and going in the cottage. If she drank, no one must know. From day to day to day, nothing much would change.

She could be respectable. Respectable, comfortable Mrs Gallwey, that lovely widow with the adorable grandson.

She had walked to the big house, found Ivan, and taken him wriggling into her lap. He had escaped and run away with Hans, the littlest of Anne-Marie's boys.

Anne-Marie had brought her a cup of tea – Beatrice was never sure whether Anne-Marie made these cups herself or whether a servant, just offstage, handed them to her on a signal – and sat beside her. 'He is welcome to stay with us, dearest,' she had said, 'even if you choose not to.' And Bea had wondered what it was in her face, her clothes, her bearing which showed that however much she pretended, she would never quite fit.

'Don't decide now,' Anne-Marie had gone on. 'Ivan is here for a visit – some fresh air, a little time with his cousins. You, I expect, must return to the city. Return later to fetch him, or to settle permanently yourself. Or if you do not —'

'It won't take him long to forget me,' Beatrice had said.

'You have given him a wonderful start in life,' Anne-Marie had said, 'but perhaps it's best for everyone if he doesn't spend any further time living in – did you say a stable? – in a stable with nothing but elderly women for company. Perhaps best for you too, dearest, not to live that way. No, don't start that again – I know you're a grown woman and you have the right to live however you see fit. Of course you do. Perhaps for once you could put your comfort ahead of your rights? Well, never mind.'

Comfort first, rights second – it was an interesting idea, she thought, as she shifted around on her chair at The Rifle Range Hotel, trying to find a spot where her behind was not assailed by splinters. This pub. The chairs, hard wood, some with the remnants of ancient leather upholstery, now largely torn away. The sticky, stained carpet with the cloth all torn where the feet most often trod. The dirt-crusted windows. She remembered that comfortable armchair, that beautiful view. She could not remember now why she had come here. It wasn't for the company – the room was empty aside from Bea and the publican. She should get a jug of beer or a bottle of gin and take it home. Back to Mrs Frome, Neddy, the empty stable. A night of quiet sleep and then tomorrow, more of the same. Perhaps a conversation with Henry Hills. If talking to a school-age child was the most she could hope for, Hahndorf probably was the superior option.

That poor family. George had come in while she was trying to decide whether to have another drink or head back to the stable. He looked drunk already, but perhaps it was the grief. She avoided catching his eye.

7

He would never be whole again. All that anger that had made him, all the pain he had felt – he saw now it was a warm bath and a cup of tea compared to this. He was dry flaking skin stretched loose over a rack of bone, shuffling from here to there and back again. A dead man in a pile of dead men, waiting to be tipped into a pit and finally given some peace.

He did not greet the publican, his old friend. He would not look at people and see that sick sweet look of sympathy crumple their faces. He asked for what he wanted and did not raise his eyes. The Gallwey woman, staring at him.

He had been trying to fix it, hadn't he? That was it. To do the right thing. His boy, his eldest, marked by evil, and he had left it too late. If he had taken the knife to him sooner, little Georgie would live still. But he hadn't had the nerve. He hadn't had the steel in him. He kept seeing the boy beneath the mark, the face like his, his mother's beautiful eyes, and he turned the blade away. Now he had one son dead and another a murderer and his wife looked likely never to rise from bed again. He clutched the thought of little Wills to him, wondered if one small boy might swim free of the wreckage.

He knew it wasn't Henry's fault. It was all his own. He had brought that thing into their homes and their lives. He had overlooked it, let it grow; in his own weakness and hubris he had nestled it in the heart of his family and let it feed from them. It had eaten the soul of one son and used it to murder the other.

Not it: she. She had eaten the soul of one of his sons. She had murdered the other. And George, fixed on his own petty suffering, had made it happen.

8

Henry would wait under the parlour window while 'Bridget' talked to his father and told him the curse was lifted. Father would be overcome with joy and he and Bridget would shake hands or perhaps embrace, and Henry could go home again. That was the idea Henry and Mark had come up with between them. But Henry had been waiting a full ten minutes now and there was still no sign of either his father or his Mark.

He'd spent twenty minutes being nervous, alert, worrying that his mother or some other relative would come down the side of the house and find him crouching there, but after half an hour the nervousness had run out and now he was throwing lumps of gravel at the apple tree to see if he could knock a piece of fruit to the ground.

A grey and white cat ran full pelt around the corner and leapt into his lap, put her paws up on his shoulder and rubbed her nose against his cheek.

'Kitty!' he said, and scratched behind the cat's ears. 'Whose kitty are you?'

The cat rubbed even more insistently.

'What? What is it?'

The cat drove her claws into his leg and he recognised, for a second, a flicker of himself in her green-yellow eyes.

'Is it you?' he whispered, and the cat purred louder than he knew a cat could purr.

She jumped off his lap and ran to the corner of the house, then sat there waiting for him. He followed her, ducking under every window, skirting every door, until they were out the front and then down the street. She held her tail high and he followed her standard the way a loyal soldier would.

'I can't go in there!' he told her, as she slipped through the door of The Rifle Range Hotel. She scampered out through the door again and led him to a spot by the back door where he could peer through a window.

Henry watched as the cat blurred itself into a lump and then once more into the form she claimed was Bridget Ledwith.

'Really?' Henry said.

'Really,' the woman replied, and this time her words sounded like words and her lips moved the way lips should move.

'You've been practising!' he said, and she curtseyed and lifted the edge of her blue-flowered skirt.

She stumbled a little on the edge of a raised cobblestone, he saw, as she tiptoed down to the pub's front door, but for the most part she looked like a slightly unsteady human woman.

Henry dragged a crate from a pile of rubbish by an outbuilding and propped it under the window. The sun was dimmed by clouds today, brighter inside the building than out, and he felt safe perched up there and watching the play unfolding before him.

Father had his head down when Bridget walked in, looking at something in the bottom of his glass. Bridget stood, swaying slightly, and Henry could see she wasn't sure where to go or what to do. The publican called out to her, 'Miss, can I help you? You shouldn't be in here,' and Henry felt shamefully relieved that she would have to go and Father would never see her and the whole plan would have to be cancelled.

'She's with me,' he heard someone say, and Bridget tottered in the direction of the voice. He pressed his face against the glass so he could see around the corner, see who was talking. Mrs Gallwey was there, and Bridget sat down on the chair beside her. Henry tried to press his face closer but he couldn't hear the words they said.

9

'Would you like a drink, dear?' Beatrice asked the very strange-looking young woman who'd stumbled into the bar. The woman nodded and Bea waited to see if she would pull a delicate purse from the folds of her terribly outmoded frock, but she didn't.

Bea went to the bar and ordered them a glass of beer each. She nodded to George Hills while she waited for the beers to be pulled, and he blearily nodded back. His head was sinking towards the table again, and it was only midafternoon. *He shouldn't be in here,* she thought. *He needs to go home, to be around that sensible wife of his. He's here too often and he's drinking too much.* Of course he was sad; of course he was destroyed. This was no way to repair it. Still, it was none of her business.

She put the glasses on the table.

'Thank you,' the woman said.

'My pleasure. Beatrice Gallwey,' Bea said, and held out her hand to be shaken. The woman took it, and her hand was limp and sandy and slightly chilled.

'My name is,' and she hesitated, 'Bridget ... Sidney. Bridget Sidney. That's my name.'

'Well, Miss Sidney, it's lovely to meet you.'

Silence sat between them.

'I was hot,' Miss Sidney said, 'and hoped to sit down for a moment.'

Bea looked out the grimy window at the rain that was just now beginning to fall from the heavy sky.

'I've found the tearoom on Military Road to be a little more sympathetic to the plight of an overheated woman,' Bea told her. 'They don't really allow ladies in here.'

'You're a lady, aren't you?' Miss Sidney asked.

'Of sorts. I haven't seen you in here before. Are you new to Port Adelaide?'

'I ... I was here before. Once. I came in a boat. No, I went in a boat. A ship. I was here and then I went in a ship and I was gone and that was the last time I was here. Yes, that's it.'

'I see. So it's been some time?'

'I suppose that's right. That would be right. Time. Time has passed, yes. Or we have passed through it. But not here. I passed through time, but elsewhere.'

'Elsewhere?'

'Yes, in another place. That's where I was.'

'And now you're back. In Port Adelaide. Where you were before – before the time passed or you, perhaps, passed through the time. Which you did somewhere else. But now you're here.'

'Exactly!' The woman grinned massively at this revelation. 'Exactly! That's it precisely!'

Silence fell again. Bea watched as Miss Sidney tried to lift her glass to her mouth. She seemed to be struggling with its slipperiness. The girl held her hand up before her face and tapped its back once, twice. A circle of flesh raised itself, pop, on her palm and she took the glass up once again, this time with great success. Her lopsided mouth broke into a grin. She took a great draught of the beer then promptly coughed it up and over her chin, into her lap.

'Gah!' she said, and poked her tongue out. 'That's beer?'

'So they say. Do you need a cloth?'

'Cloth? Oh no,' Miss Sidney said, and she stood up and shook her skirt until most of the beer had sprayed onto the surrounding tables and floor. She sat down again. 'You drink that?'

Bea nodded.

'It's a bundle of mysteries, isn't it, this world?' the woman said. 'Always something else. Horses. Sandwiches – have you tried those? Walking on two feet. Leather – it's made out of the skin of other living creatures, I found out. Singing, and sometimes everyone knows the song and they all sing too. You can take the fat from a whale and put a flame to it and then you have a light to read. Or sew – that's a thing people do. Well. And now beer.'

'And now beer. Perhaps you'd prefer gin?'

They sat quietly again for a moment, until Miss Sidney said, 'Thank you, I have to go now.'

'Well, it was lovely to meet you,' Bea said to her back, and watched as the woman took slow and tiny steps towards the door. Almost there, she turned back and stared towards the table where George Hills sat, slumped and staring. She raised a hand and waved to him, and it was the strangest thing Bea had ever seen.

The moment seemed to stretch and stretch as George sat with his chin in his hands, staring at her, and her little hand waved left, right, left, right, left, right. 'Hello, George. George, my friend,' she said.

He leapt from his chair and flung himself at her, knocking her backwards onto the floor.

'Monster, monster, monster!' he was yelling, 'what did you do to my boy? What did you do to my boy? You filthy monster, show yourself!'

'Mister Hills!' the publican said, and set about dragging himself from behind the bar, but long before he'd finished wiping his hands and tucking some glasses safely away, George was trying to tear the woman's dress from her body.

'Show yourself! Show your true self!'

'I'll get the police,' said the publican, and left the room. The woman was burbling, 'It is me! It is me! I am here to free you! It is me!'

Bea stood up to intervene, but stopped short when she saw that George's hands, rather than rending the dress's fabric, were stretching its edges into unthinkable shapes. Miss Sidney's arms were elongating as he grasped and grappled with them. Her face had sagged down on one side and her eye had taken over half her cheek. Her dark hair flickered and swarmed and Bea's brain revolted against the shapes it made.

The door swung open again and Bea looked around, dreading to see the police. This could not end well for George Hills. But instead it was the boy Henry, wet with rain and wide-eyed with shock.

'No, Father, don't!' he said. 'She has to tell you!' And he flung himself into his father's flailing arms. George's fist knocked him down – inadvertently? – and Beatrice called the boy to her side.

Miss Sidney was blurring, shifting, drooping and sliding. George's arms met more and more often with nothing as the thing that had been Miss Sidney smeared itself across the carpet, while Bea swallowed against the vomit that tried to rise in her throat. What horrible creature was this, this ball of purple sticky matter rolling across the filthy floor, coating itself in lint and grit? The thing stretched and Bea squinted to look at it. From one eye she watched as it firmed itself into the shape of a grey and white cat. The cat jumped onto the bar, to the windowsill, out the window and was gone.

'You saw it,' George said, pulling himself up from the floor. 'You saw it!' He turned to Bea. 'You saw that thing, that monster. You saw it!'

She nodded.

'And you!' he said, turning on Henry, who had leapt onto the bar himself, where he was calling through the window to the cat. 'Why are you here? What are you doing? Who are you?'

Henry turned his face to his father, his back against the wall.

'Tell me who that is,' Henry said.

'You know, you know what it is, it's part of you, you're part of it.' George leant, puffing, on the bar, half muttering and half yelling at the child.

Henry tried to shuffle back further. 'Say her name,' he said, trying to snuffle the weeping away. 'Who is she? Why is she here?'

'Mister Hills, calm down,' Bea said, but George paid her no attention.

'I don't know what she is,' he said instead. 'I summoned her. I made her, I fed her, she is the darkness of my soul made flesh. I am sorry. I'm sorry.'

George's hands went to his knees and he bent unsteadily forward, took a deep, ragged breath and then another. Then he raised himself up and shuffled to the nearest wall, leant against it.

'Come here, Henry,' he said.

'You don't have to,' Beatrice said.

Henry slid down from the bar and walked slowly towards his father. Bea picked herself up from her chair, just in case she was needed.

'I knew she was no woman. I knew it!' He called the last in Bea's direction. 'And you told me there was no such thing as haunting.'

'What?'

'You said a woman couldn't be a spirit, an evil haunting spirit, you said it was just my wounded manhood making her into something she never was. But you saw! You saw that thing!'

'I did see that thing. I did.' She walked up behind Henry and as his father leaned forward again to take a gasping breath she quickly flicked back his collar and looked at his neck. 'Yes, I see,' she murmured. 'Of course it was.' Henry slapped her hand away.

George finally sat down in his chair again. 'Henry,' he said, 'I'm not going to hurt you. Come here.'

Henry did, holding his place firm a little further away from his father than the man's outstretched arm could reach.

'Did you kill your brother?' he asked. 'Tell me now. Your mother doesn't ever need to know. No one will ever know but you and me. I know it isn't your fault – I know it was that thing. But you have to tell me.'

Henry shook his head.

'Say it. You have to say it.'

'I wish I had saved Georgie. I wish I'd believed him when he told me he was sick. I wish I hadn't asked him to come to the drain with me. I wish I hadn't sent him home to fetch supplies. I wish I had just run away and left him at home and he was happy and alive and you and Mother would forget you ever had me and just love Georgie and Wills and especially Georgie, because he was the best boy that ever lived,' and Henry burst into sobs again.

'But did you kill him?'

'I didn't kill him!' Henry yelled. 'I didn't, I didn't, I didn't. Why do you think I'm so wicked? Why can't you like me how I am?' His face was red and crumpled and spit flew from his mouth and sprayed his father's face. 'Why?'

George had nothing to say. He sat back in his chair with his face in his hands and Henry watched him weep.

'She's only small, Father,' Henry said. 'We all are,' and he reached out a hand towards his father's shaking leg. But Beatrice didn't think that George had heard.

After a while George said, 'I'm sorry.' Then, a little later, 'But you saw her, didn't you? Both of you? You saw her.'

Beatrice nodded.

The publican came back, a policeman with him.

Beatrice looked around. A man, in a chair; a boy, no longer crying, sitting on the floor at his father's feet; a middle-aged woman, not afraid, standing at a sensible distance. Nothing to see here.

'I'll take my son home,' George said, standing and offering his hand to the boy. Henry pretended not to see.

'Nothing's broken,' Bea told the publican. 'She left right after you did.'

'That child shouldn't be in here,' said the policeman.

'You're right,' said George. 'I'm taking him home now.'

'Perhaps best if you stay home for the next little while, Mister Hills.' The publican turned to the policeman. 'Sorry to bother you, Ted.'

'No problem. Is this the child's mother?' the policeman asked. Beatrice placed a protective, motherly hand on Henry's back and the three of them walked out.

'Let me get you a rum, Ted,' she heard the publican say.

'Well,' she said, once they were out of the building, 'that was a little more entertaining than I'd expected.'

'Missus Gallwey,' said George, 'would you mind … that is, could you not …'

'Don't tell anyone?'

'Don't tell anyone.'

'Good news for you, Mister Hills – I intend to sail for

Albany later this week.' From there, Colombo, then Calcutta. The world was too full of surprises: she couldn't lock herself away in a sausage shop.

10

I could have killed him. I could have. Put him in the ground with little brother, his face all bloodied. I could. That man. My first-known human. My lifelong enemy. My friend. My brother my curse.

I could do it. I could kill him right now and I could disappear and no one would ever find me.

No one has ever looked.

Who cares where I am or what I do?

I am wet, shaken and stretched. I am angry, scared. I am here all alone again alone alone alone. I am so sick of all of this, this stupid world of running and hiding and hiding and running and pretending to be someone I am not and never have been.

Here where there is no place for me. Where there is no one I know and no one who cares if I live or die. Don't get me started on Henry, he would be stupider and narrower without me and that would make him far, far happier than he is today. If he never sees me again he will live like a normal boy and grow up into a healthy man and take his place in the great parade of stomping.

Perhaps if I had made myself a man instead of a woman. But what did I know? Nothing. I knew nothing then and not much more now. Ten years, eleven, twelve, whatever it's been of hour after hour living the life of a small boy. I know bones. I know death and rotting. I know cats and fights and fear and scabs, I know trees and the treachery of other boys. I know pies in pockets; I know sweets stolen from counters when the shopkeeper's back is turned. I know mud. I know volcanoes and far-distant jungles, I know tribes who eat dirt and tribes who eat other people. Between us we know every squirm and drop of the underwater life. I know nightmares. I know my mother's hand between my shoulder blades, stroking me quietly back to sleep.

I do not know where my people are, I do not know how to live like me. But I cannot be a human boy for the rest of my life. I cannot.

I am wet. I do not care about cold but I feel cold. I am tired of every last bit of all of this.

I want to be home.

11

As they reached the pier, George slipped his hand from his son's and asked Mrs Gallwey if she would mind seeing the boy home.

'Tell your mother I'll just be a little while,' he said. 'A bit of time, and air. Just to clear my head. I won't be long.'

He took the bridge across the inlet, walked through Glanville until he reached the ocean, then headed north, the rain drenching his jacket and his hat, soaking through to his shirt, his hair dripping water freely into his eyes. His socks began to squelch inside his shoes. On the beach at Semaphore, after walking for perhaps an hour, he stripped himself clear of the clinging wet of his clothes and left them piled under the pier. He slipped into the water there, hidden from human eyes, and lay on his back in the shallows, breathing between the small waves that broke over his exposed face.

His poor boy. There was nothing he could do now, but he

would have liked to have felt Henry's skinny fingers clutched between his own one last time. He would like to think the boy might forgive him.

George's palms felt the sand shift under the tiny currents. He closed his eyes and let the water float his body, cold and old and tired. His beard, the clinging weed, they wrapped in all together and he told the ocean that was fine, they were together again now, this time he would stay. A hand slipped into his, cold and rough, and his eyes stayed closed because he knew who it was: of course, of course. Her skin coiled around his and still he lay, calm, floating, because everything between then and now had been a dream, hadn't it, dreaming he had been saved, been warm and dry, married, had children, seen his boy die; had eaten food and slept in a bed, felt his wife's hot skin beneath his, the sun on his back; that he had walked among the living. A dream of an addled, forsaken mind that clung to a wreck out of reach of humanity, still, here on Carpenters Reef. He saw it now. He knew. He opened his eyes to stare once again upon the reeking, frozen pile of ruined ship that was his eternal home and instead saw above his face the timbers of the Semaphore jetty and, wrapped around his arm and chest, the tentacles of a mythical creature: a giant blue octopus.

'Fuck Jesus!' he shrieked and grasped the tentacle in his free hand, tugging it from his skin. It would not be shifted. He thrashed about in the shallow water and the suckers clung ever tighter across his chest, the monster pulling him deeper, under the waves.

'Quiet, George,' he heard the thing say, its voice somewhere inside his head. 'Shut up and lie still and this will all be over in just a minute.'

'Help!' he cried. 'Help!'

But the thing was in his mouth, in his brain, and he could not find enough of himself still living to make a noise.

His body lay still, his mouth barely breathing, the cold water breaking over him and the only difference from that time before was that now he had no belt and not even one shoe.

'You didn't understand anything, George,' it told him, his own brain told him. 'Why were you so angry? You lived, you fool! You got to have a whole wonderful life on a beautiful world and all you could do was rage against it. I should pull you under these pitiful waves and let you drown in three inches of water. You mean nothing – nothing. None of anything that happened on that ship meant anything at all. You're a speck, a tiny speck in time, in space. Nothing. Look.'

And then the voice showed him a story.

On a planet, all ocean, there was a small, happy person living small and happy and quiet in her own small niche, her own small place, her own quiet space. Born, grew, ate, grew, lived, loved, ate. The sun, that star, shining on her one happy face.

One day they came out of the sky and her world filled up with dirt and everyone she knew died. She fought and killed and everyone else she didn't know died and everyone who was left fled. She, they, all of them tumbled into another time, space, dimension and she fell into a new ocean in a place called earth.

And she lay there under the ocean for time and time and time and time until she was brave enough and scared enough and sad enough to come out. She grabbed the first thing passing by – a boat, it turned out to be – and she made herself the first shape she saw – a woman, it was – and she made her first friend on this new planet and his name was George.

And George saw himself, there on the wreck, through the eyes of another: his exhausted, shivering, starving form, so young, and he wanted to wrap himself in his own arms, tell himself that it would all be over soon. That he would be safe. That this was nothing – just a moment – and that the rest of life stretched before him. That someone would love him. That he would wear warm socks and drink water cool from the larder. That he would sleep in a bed. That he would close his eyes and sleep in a bed and wake warm under a kind sun.

'And then off you went and off I went,' said the voice in his head, and George felt himself torn from that kind person who had looked at him and held him and kept him safe, 'and for a while I was a cat that lived near your house and you would sometimes feed me scraps, and later I was there when your boy was born, and then I came to live with you,' and George saw her, in his house, and felt the fear rise up in him again and wondered why it was.

'So many years I was there, trying to learn how to live in this world. From Henry, from you, my first-known. And all you could do was hate me and fear me and all I wanted was a place to be safe.'

George tried to remember where it had come from, all that hate.

'Show me her again,' George said.

'That Ledwith creature?'

'Yes.'

'She isn't real.'

'I know. Show her to me.'

And George watched inside his mind as Bridget Ledwith lay beside him on the *Admella*'s wreck, flickered past his upstairs window, wrestled with him on the floor of the pub not two hours ago.

'She's only me,' the voice told him.

'She's you and you're me. We're all together. Show me the journey again,' George said.

'Your sinking boat?'

'No, your journey.'

So she did. And George looked into the hearts of stars and wondered how he had been so blind to it his whole life, that there was more to his existence than just this, than homes, jobs, children, family, ocean, sky, food and shipwrecks. The fear that sucked at him: it was from out there, from the great cold blackness beyond his thin, blue sky. But when he plunged his face into that black, felt it wash over him like icy water, the fear pulsed hot joy in his skin and he felt the edges of himself smear and stretch. The great, quiet space of it. Something inside him broke open and the oily fluid that had gummed the workings of his heart spilled out and into that eternal, infinite, endless space and was gone.

He breathed.

Then, 'Where are the rest of them?' he asked.

'The rest?'

George propped himself up on an elbow to stop the water getting in his mouth. 'The ones like you. The others who left.'

'Oh.' The voice was quiet for a while. 'I don't know.'

'Well, where did they say they would be?'

'They didn't. They didn't say.'

'Here, though?' George asked.

'Port Adelaide?'

'No, this place. Earth.'

'Yes. Here. Earth.'

'Now?'

The voice went quiet again and George could feel it, just under his own mind, trying to remember.

'Because you know there used to be thousands like you,' George said, or maybe thought. 'Tens of thousands. Sailors talked about them. Sailor stories, tall stories, legends. Eight-legged creatures sliding onto becalmed ships, wrecked ships. Shifting shapes, wreaking havoc.'

'Used to?'

'The oceans were full of them.' George sat up out of the water and saw the thing had shrunk down, blended itself with his own body, and he felt calmer than he had in a very long time. 'Before my time.'

He sluiced the water from his skin and squirmed his way back into his wet clothes, covering the mark. 'One bloke told me, oh, twenty years ago, that his grandfather had seen one, transformed itself into a tiger and ate the cabin boy then slid off back into the sea. Ridiculous story.'

George thought some more. 'And in Warrnambool, a fella said he'd seen a creature in a freak show, in America, suspended in brine. A fraud, he thought – something cobbled together out of bits of fish. Still, it could've been.'

'Where did they come from? Did anyone see them come? Did anyone see?'

'They'd been here long before us. William told me. Or maybe it was Henry. That they'd been on earth longer than almost anything alive. Millions of years perhaps.' He thought for a while. 'I don't know what that means. That some creatures have existed longer than others? That the earth is old. That there were once things, millions of years ago, that there aren't anymore.'

The earth is old, he thought mostly to himself. *Older than we could ever know.* He felt himself shrink and the weight of it all tumbled off his tiny, insignificant frame.

His socks were far too wet to wear so he pulled his shoes onto his bare feet.

'And now they're gone?'

'I don't know if there's anyone alive who's ever seen someone like you.' *Except me,* he thought. *And Henry.*

'They could be hiding?'

George shrugged, but he didn't think so and neither did the thoughts in his head.

'But where did they…?'

'No one knows. One day, they were just gone.'

12

I am a million years too late.

I am a million years too late. They are gone. Home. They are gone home and I am here and I am a million years too late. A million years they were under this star, the sun: my people, then their people and all their little billions of people and now? And now, just me. Hello, where is everyone? Hello?

Gone.

Home.

I clutch around his neck, limbs about his neck and waist like a joyful piggyback-riding child and not even a molecule of joy inside me, or wait.

Wait.

One.

One molecule and it says to me this is done now, this is done. You are here. Whoever you want to be. They are gone and you are here and there is nothing more for you to do.

You are alone. No one knows you and you are alone.

I sing the song of my people and it drops frail into the dust, no other ears to hear, and this time I let it lie. The breezes of this earth raise the dust and my song blows hot across the streets and homes of this town and settles into the skin of its people, into its creatures, into the grey-green leaves of its stoic trees and settles soft over every dish of food, into every mouth that feeds.

We are here on his street now before his house, my house, and I unpeel myself and slide, soft, down the back of him, down the leg of him, from the cuff of his trousers and onto the dirt and here I am again, fleet-footed fur, and I roll in the dirt and the sun, that star, shines on my belly, and his hand strokes my belly, and I feel the flow of my hot animal blood.

'Henry,' I hear him say from inside the house. 'Henry, are you there?'

And the boy calls back and the man says, 'Henry, why don't you go into the larder and cut a slice of meat for this cat of yours?'

A NOTE ON HISTORY

On 6 August 1859, the steamship *Admella* was wrecked on Carpenters Reef, about 1 kilometer off the coast of South Australia. It had left Port Adelaide the previous day, making its regular trip to Melbourne. One hundred and thirteen people were aboard – eighty-four passengers and twenty-nine crew. For more than a week the wrecked and broken ship was stuck on the reef, its inhabitants slowly dying from hunger, thirst and exposure. Many attempts were made to rescue them, but terrible weather and bad luck meant every effort failed. Finally, the wreck was reached by a lifeboat from Portland, Victoria: twenty-four people had survived the eight-day ordeal. Among them was Bridget Ledwith (who was in all likelihood not an alien from another dimension, but whose identity was a source of mystery and controversy in the years after the wreck) and George Hills, my great-great-grandfather. George had been washed off the boat during the first moments of the wreck, but was rescued by Soren Holm, an able seaman from Denmark; Holm drowned soon after while trying to reach shore and raise the alarm.

After his rescue, George married his fiancée Eliza Ridge; they had eight children including Henry (who lived until he was seventy-three), George (or Georgie, who died when he was nine), and their youngest daughter, Sarah, who was the mother of my grandmother, Nancy Bradley. George Hills died in 1916 at the age of eighty-three. You can read his account of the wreck by searching the website Trove for George Hills, *Admella* and the Adelaide *Register*.

Other than these facts and some accounts of the wreck taken from Ian Mudie's book *Wreck of the Admella*, *From the Wreck* is entirely made up and bears no relationship at all to reality.

ACKNOWLEDGEMENTS

Thank you to my uncle Andrew Hirst for inviting me to Mount Gambier in 2009 for the 150th anniversary of the wreck of the Admella, and for making me realise this was something I wanted to write about. Thank you also to my mum, Anne Rawson, and my cousin, Catherine Hirst, who had already done so much of the research before I even started thinking about the wreck, and to mum for reading several drafts.

Thank you to those who encouraged me to write this the way I wanted to write it. Marlee Jane Ward listened to me thrash the idea out of my head and said it was something that would work. Jane Ormond, Rose Mulready and Bridget Weller have been, as always, my stalwart writing companions. Charlotte Wood and Alison Manning ran a two-day workshop that helped me get my brain in shape.

Rose Mulready, Rose Michael and Patrick Allington all

read drafts and made the manuscript so much better than it would otherwise have been. My late, much-missed uncle John Hirst fixed some of my historical errors, told me to keep going and shared many plates of cheese-on-toast. Penelope Goodes was an incredible editor with a sharp eye and a deep understanding of what I was trying to do. Peter Lo designed another brilliant, beautiful cover for my work. Barry Scott has been such a supporter of my odd tales, and publishes some of the best books in Australian literature.

Thank you to those who inadvertently inspired me: my uncle George Rawson, who endured appendicitis, two older brothers, and the terror of a fictitious tramp called Johnny Greenteeth; my nephew Tane Rawson, whose brilliant brain is a great joy; my dad, Howard Rawson, who has been telling me imaginary stories my whole life; Kat Scarlet, who made me a stunning tattoo of George Hills and the Admella and who suggested Bridget Ledwith might be creepier than I thought; Rebecca Giggs, whose Granta article 'Whale Fall' was a magnificent insight into the underwater world; and Jessie Cole, my calming, enlightening and ever-amusing pen pal.

And thank you, of course, to my husband Andy, who is amazing – he really gets why someone would bother to waste their life plugging away at a piece of art that may never matter to anyone else. He also noticed that octopuses are probably from another dimension: that was very helpful.

This book is set on the lands of the Buandig and Kaurna

people, and was written on the lands of the Boonwurrung and the Woiwurrung people of the Kulin nation.

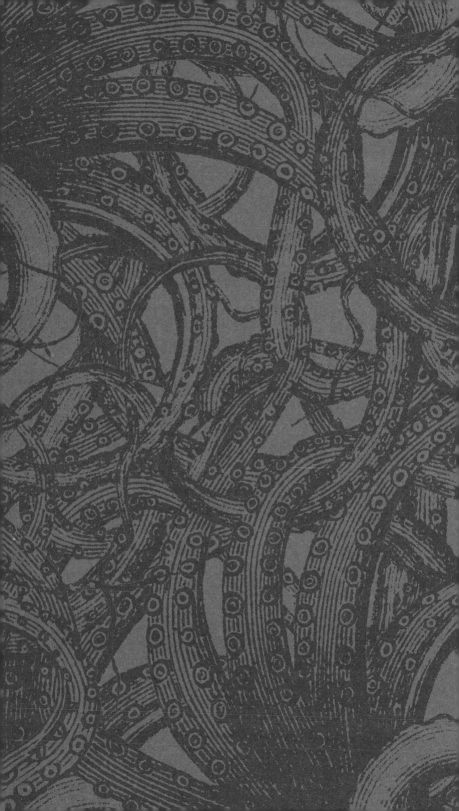